JOHN COON

Ripples in Space

Samak Press

The real challenge is to work out what aliens might actually be like.

Stephen Hawking

Contents

I

Out of Silence

By: Jean Marie Bauhaus

Out of Silence

Space walking had always been his favorite. Outside the confines of the freighter, nothing but stars as far as the eye could see. Nothing between him and the airless vacuum but a helmet and a suit. That vulnerability had always frightened Nora a little, but it invigorated him. Being alone in the vastness quieted his mind and filled him with peace.

No peace came for him now as he drifted further and further away from his freighter – his home. He wasted no oxygen on swearing, though he wasn't sure why he bothered prolonging the inevitable.

"Lucas?"

Nora's voice came over the comm, thickly accented and heavy with emotion. She sounded like herself, and he blew out a relieved sigh, filling his helmet with more carbon dioxide. He spent no breath responding. She couldn't hear him, anyway.

"Lucas, I'm sorry. I'm so sorry."

Don't be, baby, he wanted to say. *It had to be this way.*

He closed his eyes, and drifted.

* * *

They made a hell of a find. A derelict transport vessel, disabled and apparently abandoned, just floating out there waiting to be stumbled upon. And they'd been the ones to stumble.

Nora had spotted the vessel about 600 meters off their port side, looking dead in space, and came to tell him about it. No signals came from the vessel, no signs of life, and sure enough, nobody responded to comms.

So they wasted no time heading over there. They both suited up for this one, though Lucas made Nora wait in the airlock while he did an initial walk through. One could never be too careful out there. He knew she hated being left behind with no way to hear if he ran into trouble. The relief on her face when he appeared in the passage and waved her on board said much more than the sweary signs she awkwardly made through the thick gloves of her suit.

Lucas found the control room while Nora searched the rest of the ship and took inventory. Soft blue light illuminated the room from the vessel's computer screens, which still operated on auxiliary power. The main power supply had apparently been damaged, along with the engines, but enough juice remained to run life support. Still, he kept his helmet on. Who knew what had happened to the passengers and crew? One life pod was gone. Presumably, they abandoned ship after incurring damage. But, for all he knew, they'd fled from contamination or contagion.

Better safe than sorry.

The ship's log told him nothing. Apparently, providing a current report of whatever had happened hadn't been on top of the captain's mind. The ship's manifest listed four passengers and three crew members. No cargo, which was disappointing.

Still, passengers might have left behind some valuables. In any case, they could probably repair the vessel and sell it for a large enough sum to keep them going for another six months or so. Or if not, they could strip it and sell the parts.

Lucas left the control room to find his wife. Maybe she had better luck.

He passed through the mess hall and common area and entered a corridor leading to the passenger cabins and engine room. He met Nora in the corridor, heading in his direction, her face lit up with excitement.

"I was coming to get you," she signed. "You have to see this."

"Found something good? What is it?"

"Just come."

She waved for him to follow and turned back the way she came. He followed her down the corridor and through a passageway that opened into the engine room. His gaze immediately landed on what must have gotten her so worked up.

"What the…?"

Lucas walked around the structure, not taking his eyes off it for a second. They'd been building something. What, he couldn't begin to guess. The object stood about three meters tall and was two meters wide, a frame made from a jumble of parts. At the base he recognized power cells and engine parts, though they'd all been tinkered with.

"They used parts from the ship," he signed.

"I know," Nora spoke. "Look."

She pointed out open panels along the walls and on the engine that filled the back half of the room. Disconnected wires and circuits hung out of them like the guts of a disemboweled animal.

"That explains why the ship isn't running. Why the hell would they do this?"

Lucas quickly realized he was at the wrong angle for her to read his lips. He turned and signed to her, repeating what he'd said.

"I don't know." She pointed. "But what is *that*?"

Lucas hadn't missed it. He just didn't quite know how to process what he saw. Suspended in the center of the structure was an orb, about the size of a bowling ball. At first glance it resembled a giant pearl, but on closer look it reminded him more of a fire opal — a living one, with swirling and pulsating colors. Lucas felt at once drawn to its ethereal beauty and repulsed by its otherness.

"Whatever it is, it doesn't look like it belongs to these parts."

"It looks valuable," she said.

He nodded.

"That it does. Priceless, I'd say." He faced her and waved at her to look at him. "But also dangerous," he enunciated, the better for her to read his lips. "We don't know what this thing is or where it came from."

"So what do you want to do?"

Lucas looked back at the orb. It gave him a strange sensation, a tickle at the back of his mind. He suddenly felt an overpowering urge to reach out and touch it. He shook his head to snap himself out of it. Every instinct told him not to bring that thing onto his ship.

"Leave it. We'll figure it out later. What else did you find?"

Nora had found a few personal valuables in the passenger cabins, some expensive clothes, gold jewelry and personal devices they could pawn. And the kitchen was well stocked with food that hadn't expired. She found some that had been prepared and left out, with mold growth suggesting it hadn't been more than a couple of weeks since the crew had abandoned ship.

"That means someone might still come looking for it," Lucas said. "The sooner we tow it out of here, the better." He motioned back toward the corridor and started walking, signing as he went. "Let's get back. We'll disengage and then I'll go out and attach the cables, and you can drive us out of here."

"Wait," she said when they reached the mess hall. Nora ran into the kitchen and rummaged in a cupboard, then came back, brandishing a package of chocolate bars with a twinkle in her eye.

"Priorities," he signed.

"Chocolate is always a priority," she said aloud.

He couldn't argue with that.

* * *

They traveled for hours, towing the derelict behind their ship. Once they'd covered enough distance that he no longer feared interference from anyone searching for the lost vessel, Lucas unhitched the ship and re-docked his freighter. Boarding with a pair of hover carts stacked with empty crates, they split up to gather the bounty. Nora took the cabins, while Lucas plundered the kitchen.

He filled three crates with canned and freeze-dried food and dry goods, then headed off to the engine room. Lucas wanted to take another look at that weird structure and see if there was any way to salvage those power cells. If not, they'd have to head to the nearest outpost soon to recharge their own batteries.

He found Nora standing in front of the structure, too damn close for his liking, and staring at the orb. She had taken her helmet off. Carefully, doing his best not to sneak up and startle her, he edged into her line of vision and waved. But she didn't notice, too transfixed by the swirling orb. He glanced at it long enough to see a pulsating kaleidoscope of colors moving in a steady rhythm that echoed his own pulse.

Lucas jerked his eyes away and waved a hand in front of her face. Nora snapped out of her trance and looked at him, her expression angry.

"What are you doing?" she signed.

He signed the same question right back, with an emphasis on *you.*

"Where is your helmet?" he added.

"My oxygen was running low. The air here is fine."

"We don't know that. You should have gone back to replace your oxygen. That's the protocol."

"I was going to."

"Then why didn't you?"

Her brow wrinkled with uncertainty, and she looked at the orb again. He touched her chin and directed her gaze back to him.

"I don't know," she said aloud. "I can't remember."

The uneasy feeling he'd gotten at first sight of the orb intensified.

"Let's get you out of here."

"Why can't I remember?"

"I don't know. You're probably just tired, but we'll run a diagnostic to be sure. I think it's time to call it a day."

She nodded and let him guide her back to the ship.

* * *

He stood on a cliff, overlooking a wide valley. A field of crystalline fauna spread out beneath him, reaching to distant pink and purple mountains, more massive than any he had ever seen or read about. Three white moons hovered above them, impossibly close and huge, suspended in a purple sky, all waxing gibbous. Beyond them, the stars arranged themselves in unfamiliar constellations.

A breathtaking view filled him with an ache of intense longing, seeding a home sickness like he'd never felt during his military service or his subsequent life of exile. He wanted to cry.

Lucas choked awake with a sob. Realizing his face was wet, he sat up and mopped his eyes and cheeks with the tail of his t-shirt. Looking down to gauge how deeply Nora was sleeping, he found her bunk empty. Lucas called out for the lights to turn on and looked around. The door to the head was open and the light was off. He picked his wrist communicator up from the shelf next to his bunk and sent a vibration to hers. A buzz from below told him she hadn't taken it with her. With a groggy sigh, Lucas pushed back the sheet and climbed out of bed.

He found Nora in the lounge, curled up on the couch and bent over her sketch pad. Her hand guided the colored pencil in her hand with a swiftness that always amazed him. In another life, another time, she would have been a celebrated artist. Lucas choked down the bitterness he always felt whenever he was reminded of the times they actually lived in, how technological progress had resulted in a regression of how humans treat each other. Sure, the worthy and the elite enjoyed a pure utopia reserved for those who were both compliant and genetically up to snuff.

For the rest, the disabled and the diseased and the deplorable, a bitter life of exile awaited, scrabbling for survival in the outer reaches of the solar system.

Could be worse, he reminded himself, thinking of the camps and cleansing campaigns he'd seen played out in Earth history holos. The people in charge nowadays believed themselves to be compassionate and benevolent by sending the undesirables deeper into space, allowing them to start their own colonies and make their own way.

At least out here, we're free.

He circled around to give Nora plenty of time to notice him coming and sat on the opposite end of the couch.

"Can't sleep?" he asked when she glanced up at him.

She shook her head and laid her sketch pad down between them.

"Bad dream."

"Yeah, me too." He glanced down at what she'd been drawing, and his heart stopped. He turned it around for a better look. "Where did you see this?"

"In my dream."

His eyes roved over the giant mountains and moons, and he shivered. Lucas locked eyes with Nora.

"I dreamed about this, too."

The edges of her mouth pulled down as a small wrinkle formed between her eyebrows. She stared at the drawing.

"What does it mean?"

"I don't know."

"Do you think it could have something to do with that…"

Her voice trailed off. He didn't need her to finish.

"I don't know," he repeated. "But I wouldn't be surprised."

A tear slid down Nora's cheek, and she swiped at it angrily.

"Hey," he said, reaching for her hand. "It's okay. We ran the diagnostics, and you were fine."

She pulled her hand away to sign.

"It's not that."

"Then what?"

Her eyes squeezed shut, and she shook her head.

"Did you feel it?" she asked aloud, looking at him. "The sadness?"

"Yeah. I felt it. It felt like…"

"Home sickness."

"Yeah. I've never felt anything like it before."

"I have." More tears welled up and escaped. "After my parents surrendered me."

Now Lucas squeezed his eyes shut.

"Oh, baby," he sighed, again taking her hand.

She'd been five years old when the mandate went out. Nora's parents could either submit to an experimental nanite injection that promised to repair her genes and restore her hearing or surrender her to a program. The program promised to train her in speech and communication and also provide vocational training. Not trusting the injection and being against the idea of genetic manipulation, her parents chose the program. Lucas couldn't say he wouldn't have done the same thing in their place.

"C'mere."

He moved the sketch to the coffee table and pulled her to him. She nestled against him and for a few minutes they just held each other. Then she pushed away and sat up to face him.

"Do you miss your old life?"

"No." He didn't hesitate. "Not one bit."

Lucas read the skepticism in her eyes.

"You were a war hero," she said. "You could be back there, with your friends and family—"

"*You're* my family," he insisted. "And my best friend."

She smiled a little at that.

"But you could have had a good life."

"Everything good in my life is right here," he said, suppressing a sigh. This wasn't the first time they'd had this conversation. Marrying her had meant leaving behind status and privilege and being consigned to a life of exile in the outer darkness. "I didn't leave behind anything that matters."

"But you could've –"

"Stop."

Lucas both spoke and signed for emphasis. He knew where she was going. What the government hadn't disclosed to her parents about the program was that it included sterilization. As soon as Nora had reached puberty, her womb had been taken from her, to prevent her from passing on her supposedly defective genes. Children were an impossibility, and he knew that ate at her much more than it did him.

"It doesn't matter," Lucas reassured her. "Not to me."

More tears. Lucas cupped her face in his hands and used his thumbs to wipe them away. Looking into her eyes, he enunciated clearly, "You're my home." He kissed her tenderly, then rested his forehead against hers, as if the contact could transmit how much he loved her directly into her brain.

"I love you," she said.

He leaned back so she could see.

"I love you, too." He stood up and held a hand out to her. "Now let's go back to bed."

"I'm not sleepy."

"Who said anything about sleep?" Lucas asked, winking at her. A sly smile graced Nora's lips, and she took his hand.

* * *

Lucas whistled to himself as he stepped over the airlock and onto the salvaged vessel. He'd left Nora curled up in his bunk, looking too peaceful to disturb. He'd showered and then made her breakfast and coffee, leaving it for her with a note telling her where he'd gone. He still wanted a good look at those power cells. And it was also time to confront the problem of the orb head on.

He'd made up his mind, though the decision hadn't been easy. The orb was undoubtedly valuable. It could probably snag them a small fortune through legal channels, and a much larger one on the black market. But it also struck him as dangerous. Lucas felt certain it had been the cause of their shared dream, if only because nothing else could explain it. And thinking about the effect it had on Nora made him all too ready to throw the orb out an airlock.

He reached the engine room and stopped cold. Nora knelt before the orb and its structure, still wearing her night clothes. Bent forward, hunched over her sketch pad, she scribbled furiously, oblivious to his presence. Sheets of paper littered the floor around her and, as he approached, he saw they were covered with strange, alien-looking symbols.

Lucas was about to walk into her field of vision when suddenly she sat up, and he stopped. Her head snapped around to look at him, as though she'd heard him behind her.

"Nora?"

She opened her mouth to speak. What came out was no language he'd ever heard. His heart hammered in his chest even as his stomach sank.

"Nora!" he barked, signing simultaneously, hoping to snap her out of it.

She stopped, and frowned, her expression puzzled. Nora tilted her head at him in a way that made him think of his childhood dog. Her lips moved again.

"Nor-ah."

The word rang out clearly in her own voice but spoken as if by someone who'd had perfect hearing and diction all their life. Lucas swallowed hard and held his hands up as he moved in front of her.

"Nora," he said as he went. "That's my wife."

He crouched before her.

"Can you hear me?"

Nora's face went blank, her eyes moving back and forth, as though processing the question.

"Can you understand me?"

Her eyes fixed on his. Nora's eyes. But she did not appear behind their gaze.

"Yes."

"Who are you?"

Again, her expression and eye movement reminded him of an ancient computer forced to buffer as it processed data. She opened her mouth again, and a string of unintelligible sounds and syllables came out. One of them sounded like Rex.

"Okay. Rex. I would like to speak with my wife. Can you make that happen?"

"Nora."

"Yes. Let me talk to Nora. I need to know that she's okay."

"Nora… no… sound. Hear." She touched her ears. "I repair." She looked over at the structure and pointed. "Repair. Not finished." She then looked down at the papers and waved a hand toward them. "You help."

"No. Not until I talk to her."

"You talk… you help?"

"It's gotta be a joint decision. If she's okay and she's on board, then we'll see."

"Help… home."

Lucas nodded, remembering his dream.

"Yeah. I kind of gathered."

Her eyes rolled back in her head and fluttered. He'd had a kid brother who'd had petit mal seizures, before his parents went for the nanite injection. This looked exactly like one of those.

Suddenly, Nora looked normal again, and slightly bewildered.

"Lucas?"

She sounded like herself again.

"Nora?"

Her hands went to her ears.

"Say something else."

"I love you." Lucas signed so she would have no doubt what he said.

Amazement spread over her features.

"Say it again."

He did. Nora broke into a grin.

"I hear you. Lucas, I can hear!"

She dove into his arms and wrapped her own around him. Lucas held her, his head swirling with thoughts and emotions too mixed up and complex to name.

"That's great, baby," he said, stroking her hair. "That's really great."

* * *

"What do you remember?"

They sat at the table in the mess room, back on their own ship. Nora drank coffee. Lucas drank something considerably stronger, contraband courtesy of one of his old Navy buddies. She stared into her mug as he spoke, and it felt strange, being able to talk to Nora without her looking at him.

"All of it," she said. "I woke up with this voice in my head. It sounded…" She signed, "Beautiful."

Nora told him it had filled her head with images and symbols, so she grabbed her sketch book and began recording them. But the more she wrote and drew, the more she felt compelled to return to the engine room.

"Do you know what they mean?"

She nodded.

"Instructions for completing the structure, and coordinates." Nora looked up at him. "It wants to go home."

"I know."

"We have to help."

Did they?

Lucas wasn't so sure. Of course she wanted to help. Nora was kind to a fault. Her grandparents owned a poultry farm when she was little, and when she'd found out what they did with the chickens, she'd cried for days before swearing off meat. She'd been a lifelong vegetarian as a result. Not that meat was available anymore. Not legally, at any rate.

Lucas, having never met a slab of bacon he wouldn't cheerfully stuff into his own maw, still favored blasting that damned orb out the airlock. The only thing stopping him was not knowing what that might do to her.

"Lucas?"

He leaned forward, placing his elbows on the table.

"Is it still in there?"

At her confused look, he reached over and tapped her head.

"Can you sense it?"

She nodded. "It's waiting."

"Can you communicate with it?"

"Yes. But I can't read its thoughts, if that's what you're thinking."

"But can it read yours?"

She frowned, considering. Signing, she said, "I don't know."

"Ask what happened to the crew." She slumped a little and shot him an exasperated look. "Don't you think that's an important question?"

She sighed and nodded. Leaning back in her chair, she closed her eyes. In a moment, her face went slack, and he had to fight the urge to grab her and shake her awake. But then she began to speak – or rather, Rex spoke through her.

"They helped. But there was not enough power. So they left."

"Why did they leave?"

"To get more power. But they did not return."

Nora's eyes opened, and she looked at Lucas. In her normal way of speaking she said, "They abandoned him." The compassion and indignation in her voice made him feel a stab of guilt for not caring more about this thing. He might have, if it hadn't hijacked his wife. And how did they know it was telling the truth?

"It's a *he* now?"

She shrugged. "That's the sense I get."

He sighed. "I don't know about this, babe."

"Lucas—"

"I don't trust this thing."

"Lucas. I can *hear.*"

He blew out a long sigh and took a long drink. That thing was still in her. It had healed her deafness. As wonderful as that may be, he couldn't shake his reservations. What else might that thing be doing to her? If it could repair her hearing, what was to stop it from shutting off her heart?

"Lucas?"

His glass now empty, he set it on the table.

"Okay," he said.

It wasn't like he had a choice.

* * *

They worked all day and into the night. At first, he had done most of the work while Nora instructed and supervised, translating her notes and passing along additional instructions from Rex. Lucas wasn't sure exactly what they were building, but he thought they were making good progress. The steel frame was fleshed out, so to speak, with more circuitry and salvaged parts from the transport ship.

But they must not have been going fast enough, because by late afternoon, Rex took control.

"This is more efficient," he said, his English getting better by the hour.

Lucas became nothing more than an occasional helping hand as Rex-in-Nora fiddled with the wiring and hooked the device into the ship's control grid.

They worked non-stop. When dinner time rolled around, Lucas's stomach growled, alerting him to the fact that they hadn't eaten since breakfast.

"You have to let her stop and eat," he told Rex.

"She has no need. I am sustaining her."

"No, she *does* have a need. She's human. She needs food, and also water. She hasn't had anything to drink since you took her over."

Now that Lucas thought about it, she hadn't even stopped to pee.

Rex kept working as if Lucas's words meant nothing to him.

"I am sustaining her," he repeated. "We must keep working."

"Why the rush?"

Not that Lucas himself didn't feel a sense of urgency to get this done and get this thing out of Nora and away from their ship. But there had to be time to rest.

"It is difficult to explain so that you will understand."

"Try."

"It will take too long. Suffice to say that there is a… a *window.* Do you understand wormholes?"

"I'm familiar with the concept."

"A wormhole is connecting our galaxies. This device will allow me to access it."

"You're opening a portal."

"Yes. One through which I may return home. But the wormhole will not remain open much longer, and I have already lost time."

Lucas nodded.

"Okay. Be that as it may, Nora still needs to eat. At least let me bring her something."

The alien assented. Nora surfaced long enough to eat a meal bar, drink some water, and assure Lucas that she was okay.

"I'm beginning to see some of his thoughts," she said. "Just flashes, images here and there."

"Anything I should know about?"

She shook her head as she chewed and swallowed.

"Mostly visions of home. It's a really beautiful planet. So other-worldly."

"Yeah, well, the sooner we can send him there, the better."

Rex wasn't so accommodating when it came to letting her sleep. No matter how much Lucas argued, the alien wouldn't budge. Unable to keep his own eyes open and unwilling to leave his wife alone with this thing, he dragged a mattress out of one of the passenger cabins and made a pallet for himself in a corner of the engine room. As Rex-in-Nora kept working, Lucas drifted to sleep.

He stood on the cliff, overlooking the valley. The sun had risen, and the last of the moons was setting behind the mountains. The crystalline jungle below was alive with color, swirling and pulsating, as if the colors themselves were living creatures. He moved closer for a better look. Peering down, he realized he wasn't standing, but hovering, with no legs beneath him. He turned. Next to him was a cliff face, made of crystal, highly reflective. He gazed at the orb as it gazed back at him.

A nudge woke Lucas out of the dream. Nora stood over him.

"I need more power."

Her perfect diction told him it was Rex speaking.

Lucas sat up and rubbed the sleep from his face.

"I'll see what I can do."

"Your ship. It has power."

"Yeah…"

"I have done the calculations. A single power cell is sufficient to operate life support and vital systems."

Lucas huffed out a laugh.

"Yeah. But we wouldn't be able to go anywhere."

"I calculate an 87.643 percent chance that another ship would respond to your distress signal within five days."

"Oh, really? What are the odds that whoever responds won't be pirates or a rival salvage crew?"

Rex remained silent.

"I'm not giving you our power cells. Let's see if there's a way to boost what you've already got."

"There is none. It is insufficient. Your ship's power cells are required."

Lucas rose to his feet.

"Look, Rex, I don't think you understand—"

"It is you who do not understand. I possess your wife."

That stopped him cold. His eyes narrowed.

"Is that a threat?"

"You will bring me the cells if you want no harm to come to her."

A stream of curse words ran through Lucas's head.

"Let me talk to her."

"I will not."

He huffed again and ran a hand over his face.

"Nora, can you hear me?"

"She can hear you, but she cannot speak. I control her vocal systems."

Lucas stared in disbelief. He vibrated with fury, but his hands were tied. There wasn't a single thing he could do that wouldn't hurt Nora.

"Fine. One cell."

"One may not be sufficient."

"One is all we can spare."

Let it be enough, Lucas pleaded with any powers that might be listening as he returned to his ship. Disconnecting the cell was a simple enough job, once he rerouted the vital systems to the backup power. Lifting the cell was usually a two-man job, but he managed, nearly throwing his back out in the process. He wrestled it onto a hover cart and returned to the transport ship.

Nora lifted the cell from the cart like it weighed no more than a small child. Lucas swallowed at the sight of her enhanced strength, and his blood ran cold as he wondered what other changes Rex had worked within her body. She set the cell at the base of the structure and then stood back to ponder it. With her hands behind her back, it took a moment for Lucas to realize they were moving.

She was signing.

His heart sped up at the realization. Lucas was so elated to see Rex didn't have total control of her that he almost missed what she was saying.

"He's lying. He doesn't want to go home. He wants to bring more of his kind here. Legions. You have to stop him." Her hands paused a moment, and then she added, "You have to destroy the orb."

She suddenly raised her hands and stared at them, then turned around and looked from her hands to Lucas.

"She speaks with her hands," Rex said.

Lucas said nothing.

"What did she say?"

He licked his lips.

"She said I shouldn't worry. That I should trust you."

Her head tilted, and then her face went slack as her eyes fluttered. It only lasted for a second, and then her gaze sharpened.

"You speak false."

Moving so fast he didn't see it coming, she backhanded him hard enough to knock him off his feet. Time expanded, stretching like a band as he flew through the air. It snapped back as he landed hard, sliding across the slick floor. Too stunned to register pain, he raised his head to see her lurching after him. Rage distorted her face, but as one half of her body dragged itself forward, the other half seemed to fight the motion, trying to pull back.

That's it. Fight him, baby.

But it turned into a losing battle as she gained both speed and coordination. Faced with the prospect of fighting his own wife — and probably getting his ass kicked, if not killed, in the process — he scrambled to his feet and ran.

He reached his own ship and closed the airlock behind him. She reached it just as it locked in place. Peering at her through the window, he engaged the lock. She raised her left hand and spelled out, "Run!" just before her right hand slammed into the glass. Lucas backed up as she hit it again, causing a hairline crack to spread.

"Shit."

He turned and raced to the control room. Behind him, glass shattered. Lucas pushed himself to run harder, faster, reaching the control room and locking himself inside. He went to set a course for the nearest space station, but with only one power cell, they didn't have enough juice to make it that far. He activated the distress beacon instead and jumped as a loud bang reverberated through the door.

As Rex kept pounding on the door, hard enough to dent it inward, he wasn't afraid for himself as much as he was afraid of what that raw physical power was doing to Nora. Not to mention what it would do to her if this thing used her own body to kill him. That would destroy her. He couldn't let that happen. He moved to stand beside the door. Flattening himself against the wall, he waited.

The door buckled, breaking its seal. The alien gripped it around the edges, pried it all the way open, and then climbed inside. Moving as fast as he could manage, Lucas grabbed his wife's body from behind, snaking an arm around her neck and grabbing her in a choke hold. Driven by the hostile force, she slammed him backward into the wall, hard enough to knock the wind out of him.

She did it again.

Again.

Somehow, he held on.

Rex clawed at his arm, even as Nora's left hand lifted and spelled out, "Kill me." Lucas prayed he wouldn't have to go that far. Squeezing tightly, he felt the strength ebbing from her body. She went still and slumped at last, and he gently lowered her to the floor and checked her pulse.

It felt steady.

Relief lasted only an instant before becoming rage. He heard himself screaming as thoughts and visions that weren't his own filled his head. His own body flung itself backward, and his limbs flailed. Lucas fought with everything he had to bring them under control. The assault on his mind felt like his head was splitting in two, but he could sense Rex's frustration as the alien struggled to integrate with his own mind and body.

Lucas regained control, but he didn't know how long it would last. Quickly, he knelt next to Nora and cradled her head in his arms.

"C'mon, baby, wake up," he said, gently slapping her face.

Her eyes fluttered and then focused on him.

"Lucas?"

Nora's speech sounded thick and distorted, and it was the most gorgeous sound he'd ever heard.

"We don't have much time," he said, helping her up.

She looked at him, stricken.

"I can't hear you," she signed.

Closing his eyes, he sighed. Lucas could only imagine her anguish, but no time remained to help her through it.

"I'm sorry," he signed. "But I need you to focus. Go get the orb and meet me at the starboard airlock."

She stared at him, hesitant and uncertain. A buzzing sound encased him as electric tentacles wormed their way around his brain.

"Hurry!" he said.

She took off. Staggering as he fought for control, Lucas made his way to the airlock. He considered as he went, struggling to think through all the options and their outcomes even as he battled against Rex's attempts to take control of him. None of the options were good. Only one would keep Nora safe.

That made his choice easy.

Lucas had already donned the suit by the time she reached him, carrying the orb. It had gone dormant without Rex to animate it, no colors, just a pearlescent white.

"What are you doing?" she asked aloud.

"Remember the plan if anything happens to me," Lucas said. "Get to Neptune base and find my buddy Ben. He'll see that you're taken care of."

She shoved the orb at him to free her hands.

"Nothing will happen to you. Just throw that thing outside!"

"It's not that simple. He's in me now."

Nora shook her head. Lucas pushed the orb back into her hands so he could take her face in his.

"I have to be quick," he said. "He's trying to take me over. Destroy that thing he built to make sure none of his friends can come through it. If you can, return the power cell so you can fly out of here. If not, someone should answer your beacon soon. You'll be fine until then."

"No! You can't—"

He pressed his lips to hers, cutting her off. Lucas would have to let go to tell her that he loved her and he didn't want to do that until the last possible second, so he tried to pour it all into his kiss. Nora sobbed against him, and he kissed her tears as they streamed down her cheeks.

Then his hands slid around her throat and squeezed.

"No!"

Lucas screamed as Rex's rage and desperation flooded his brain. But he was desperate, too, and he held on for dear life to the love he felt for his wife, who stared back at him, her eyes filled with fear as she gasped for breath and clawed at his hands.

"Let… her… *go!*"

He gained control of his right hand and used it to pry his left off Nora. Once she was free, he pushed her out of the airlock, grabbed the orb from her, and rolled it across the floor to the outer door.

"Lucas!" she screamed as he slammed the door shut, sealing her out and him inside.

Nora pounded on the glass, her normal strength ineffectual against it. Wasting no time, Lucas put his helmet on and locked it in place.

Then he took one last look at his wife.

Open the door. Break her neck and proceed to the other ship. The others are waiting. We must activate the portal.

"Like hell," Lucas said.

He opened the outer door, and watched Nora shrink from him as he flew backwards into space.

***

Lucas closed his eyes, and drifted.

"Lucas…"

The longing, the frustration, the grief in her voice over the comm all melded together into a sharp edge that rent his heart in two.

"I don't know… I want…" The signal wasn't breaking. Her voice was. "Shit!"

Lucas laughed, in spite of everything, even as tears streamed down his face. That about summed it up.

"I don't know how to do this without you."

You will, baby. You'll figure it out, I know it.

She kept talking, but the signal started breaking up. He was drifting out of range. What snatches made it through sounded like they were underwater. Or he was. Gray fingers reached and danced around the edges of his vision as his lungs labored to drink in every last drop of air. But he saw the orb, now a distant dot, alive and swirling, floating away to be someone else's problem.

Lucas had done his part. His wife was safe.

I love you.

He wasn't sure whether he heard her say it, or whether he simply thought it. But it was the last thing to penetrate his consciousness before it faded to black.

* * *

He stared at the orb reflected in the crystalline cliff face. Color swirled and pulsed over the surface of his skin in rhythm with the jubilation he felt. He was not alone. Behind him, hundreds, thousands of his own kind, their minds and their emotions and their colors in sync with his own. He turned to face them. They had come to send him off on his mission. He, among so many so much like him, had been chosen for this. To seek out new hosts. To prepare the way. He felt proud, but also afraid. He would be cut off from the collective.

He would be alone.

The orb drifted through space, cut off from his hosts, cut off from his race. He had failed.

But there would be other ships. Other hosts. Other windows.

And he had time.

Jean Marie Bauhaus has had a lifelong love affair with horror, science fiction, and fairy stories. A writer of spooky and suspenseful tales, she's the author of seven novels and counting, along with an increasing number of novellas and short stories. A ginger GenXer born and raised in Oklahoma, she currently makes her home in the middle of the woods deep in the Ozark mountains of Arkansas with her husband and best friend of 18 years and an ever-growing menagerie of animals. You can find her and her fiction on Substack @jeanmariebauhaus and learn more about her books at jeanmariebauhaus.com.

II

Tract 16

By: Christopher W. McGuiness

Tract 16

olly ran off.

Anna wasn't surprised. Old Mol' was a dyed-in-the-wool cattle dog, used to roaming for miles around the ranch's vast tracts of land. She hadn't adjusted well to being dragged inside the house. After so much freedom, it must have seemed downright claustrophobic to the poor mutt.

Molly was curled up on the sofa when Anna went to open the front door and peek outside. In the blink of an eye, the salt-and-pepper shepherd mix dashed past her at top speed, leaped over the gate, and disappeared into the wide expanse of wild New Mexico desert.

Once upon a time, Anna could have stopped her dog's daring escape, but unlike old Molly, her reflexes were slower than they'd once been. All she could do was frantically call Molly's name as the dog shrank into a jittering dot between the red-brown earth and the cloud-spattered sky. She shut the door and had a good, hard cry before drying her eyes and taking a deep breath. She resigned herself to the fact she'd have to trek into property.

Anna dressed wordlessly in battered hiking boots, jeans, and a loose-fitting chambray shirt. She stuffed a canvas backpack with water and provisions, then grabbed the old M16 rifle leaning against the wall near the back door. The gun once belonged to her Uncle Coco— a souvenir from the first Gulf War. An old rifle, but well-maintained. Oiled and glistening black. Her fingers ached as she loaded the magazine.

Hurts to load a gun. Hurts to open a jar. Hands are gonna' be damn useless before I know it.

Anna shouldered the pack and slung the gun across her back. She pulled her hair, streaked with gray, back in a utilitarian ponytail so tight it tugged at the skin of her temples. Anna grabbed a dirt-smeared Stetson from the nail by the door and placed it on her head before stepping outside. No need to consult a map. Anna knew every square inch of the ranch. Large as the property was, it didn't take a genius to know where Molly had run off to.

Tract 16.

These days, it was always Tract 16.

Up until a few years ago, the ranch had been a cattleman's paradise. Acre upon acre of grazing land nestled between the northern Rio Arriba County line and the Colorado border. It had been in Anna's family going back uncounted generations. Every inch was prime land except Tract 16. Located on the southwest corner of the ranch, the acreage consisted of nothing but desert wasteland littered with craggy ridges and strange rock formations. Nothing out there but dirt, snakes, and cacti.

And the Wobble.

* * *

Anna stopped for her first sip of water three miles into her hike. Then, pushing aside limp strands of rusted barbed wire on a half-hearted fence, she started down a worn footpath into Tract 16. She entered a barren vista pockmarked with jagged cliffs and crooked hoodoos that seemed to defy gravity. Even before the Wobble, the place had a poor reputation. Bad land, sour soil, and according to her late Uncle Coco, cursed.

The sun beat down on Anna as she walked. She came to an open space littered with bleached bones. They were remains of the ranch's last cattle. Those cows had wandered away from their grassy pastures to this place of scarcity and death, lured by the Wobble. Its power drew creatures great and small. She couldn't even enjoy the utility and company of a horse on this rescue mission. A truck would have been just as nice, but the Wobble was equally tough on engines. They either stalled or exploded once the vehicles hit the edge of Tract 16. Anna had learned this the hard way. So, she walked and her boots ground the ossified skeletons to a fine dust. The sun shone directly overhead when she stopped for another rest. Anna took a long swig from her canteen and pulled a little notepad from the breast pocket of her shirt. The date and time of her departure were scrawled on the paper, along with several basic facts about her morning.

When I woke, there was a bug crawling on the windowsill. Beetle.

Breakfast. Coffee in blue cup (cracked). Burned the eggs. Gave them to Molly.

Molly ran off.

She tried to memorize each phrase. Time got slippery the closer you got to the Wobble. The words were her anchor — a lifeline to keep her from losing herself.

"All for a damn dog," Anna muttered.

She moved on, putting a few more miles on her boots. The big sky pressed down on her and shadows grew longer. Hoodoos marked the path forward like lifeless, crooked sentinels. The whole landscape seemed to lean toward her, funneling Anna further out into Tract 16's wild desolation.

Ever closer to the Wobble.

* * *

"The curse and the gold were here long before our family laid claim to this land," Uncle Coco said.

They were camping on a flat ridge overlooking Tract 16. Anna was nine, and her uncle had taken her out hunting. She'd bagged a single, scrawny rabbit and they sat in the star-splattered dark cooking the carcass over a small fire. Coco grinned as the flames wavered in his eyes. He was deep into a bottle Ten High and in a congenial mood. Primed to tell dirty jokes, ghost stories, and dark truths to Anna, who was the only blood relative he seemed able to tolerate.

"Oñate was on the warpath and needed to stash some of his gold, but he couldn't be bothered with doing the dirty work himself," Coco continued. "He sent a detachment of soldiers out here to bury it, but they found a whole damn Indian village parked right here on this very spot. Couldn't have that. So, the Spaniards waited until night and bushwhacked em'. Killed 'em all. Men, women, and children."

Anna, equal parts terrified and entranced, leaned in closer. The flames of the fire warmed her cheeks and lips.

"When it was done, the soldiers left their heads in a big pile right in the middle of the desert," Coco gestured out into the creeping dark beyond the camp's lighted oasis. "Just over there."

Anna looked away from her uncle's grizzled face and into the stygian night, sure she could feel the dreadful miasma of the curse lurking just outside the ring of the fire's light.

"There's a curse in the soil out there, Anna. All that bad blood soakin' into the ground for years and years and years. Soaking down into the land and the gold."

She asked him, wide-eyed, why he wanted to find treasure if it was cursed. Coco winked, took another pull from the bottle, then offered it to her. Anna grabbed it, took a tentative sip, and then quickly gave it back to him, coughing as a few meager drops of liquid fire ran down her throat.

"Don't you worry about your old uncle, kiddo," Coco said as he took the bottle back. "I've got it all figured out. Gonna' get my ass to town and go to mass. Sneak some holy water out in a little bottle. I'll hit that gold with it and say a little prayer. Poof goes the curse."

He grinned and touched his index finger to his temple. Anna smiled, relieved. She felt the fire's comforting heat and rocky ground under her sleeping bag's soft fabric. She also felt a swelling sense of pride in her uncle and his plan. She felt—

I burned the eggs. Molly ran off.

Anna staggered back, rubbing her temples. It wasn't night. She wasn't nine and her uncle was many years dead and there was no gold and no curse. Just the Wobble muddying her thoughts.

"Damn."

Anna spat in the dirt. She hadn't expected the Wobble to be this strong so few miles into the tract. It confirmed her growing suspicion that it was expanding.

A noise in the distance. It might have been the wind, or maybe a muted bark. Hard to tell. Anna picked up her pace, steeling her mind against further trickery from the Wobble.

* * *

Another half mile in, she found the first carcass. All that was left of the creature were a few crablike legs, broken shards of its spiny shell, and a grayish pulp of unidentifiable organs strewn in a wide circle. A fetid, salty smell hung in a cloud over the ruin. Anna battled her gag reflex and kicked over a shattered piece of the thing's carapace. Another varmint from the Wobble. She pictured Molly, the ugly critter firmly clenched in her jaws, shaking her shaggy head from side to side as otherworldly guts flew into the hot desert air like party streamers. Anna wondered if it had toxic blood. She was used to picking off the odd fauna that wandered out of the Wobble from a safe distance but had thus far been lucky enough to avoid any close encounters. Anna called Molly's name but got no answer. She saw no signs of mammalian blood or fur and that gave her a small measure of hope.

Anna followed the trail of viscera and wondered how many of the critters had escaped her notice. She worried that one day something truly nasty might make its way off her land and into town.

A flash of brilliant, blinding white greeted her eyes. The next thing she knew, Anna lay on her back staring up at the endless azure sky. She couldn't move, but her neck was cocked at an odd, impossible angle, allowing her to stare down at her chest. Yellowing exposed ribs poked out from the tattered scraps of her shirt. She knew, somehow, she was dead. Left as food for all the skittering abominations crawling around Tract 16. Anna felt a deep crack in the back of her skull. The blow that ended her life. She felt sunlight pouring through the empty sockets where her eyes used to be.

Coffee in a blue cup. The cup had a crack. I ain't dead!

Anna hurled back her body with a jolt. She lost her balance, falling backward and landing flat on her back in the dust. Her head narrowly missed a massive rock jutting out of the bone-dry earth. The impact stole air from her lungs, and she lay struggling to catch her breath, wheezing out a stream of words her late father would have called "unladylike".

Anna tossed and turned on her back like a turtle trying to right itself. The heavy rucksack dug into her spine. Her arms were hopelessly tangled in the rifle's strap. She was almost too distracted trying to get back on her feet to notice the off-rhythm chittering of something approaching.

It skittered out from behind a rock outcropping less than ten feet from Anna's prone body. Her eyes went wide when she saw it. A crab-like thing the size of a large house cat, likely a sibling or a mate of whatever Molly had killed. Like everything else that came from the Wobble, it looked *wrong*. The crab-thing lumbered drunkenly on an uneven number of segmented legs, waving a single claw covered in black, insectoid eyes. A puckered, fleshy mound rose like a volcano between the thick plates on its back. Anna could smell its deep-sea reek as it crawled toward her.

Anna slid off her pack and sat up. The thing was as fast as it was clumsy. She dug the heels of her boots into the ground and tried to push herself away from its advance, dragging the M16 along by its sling. The eye-covered claw reached out, snapping at the air just inches from her foot. She grunted and gave the creature a hard kick. There was a stomach-churning crunch as the brittle shell around the claw gave way, sending flesh, eyes, and a dark jet of ichor flying into the air.

"Scram, goddammit!"

The crab-thing was not deterred. It lurched back to its feet, wheeling blindly back toward Anna. The lump on its back opened, and the wet fissure expelled a mass of thin, pinkish strands. There were dozens of them, fine as hair, wet and quivering. Each strand drifted toward the ground, spreading out in all directions. A few landed on Anna's right boot. She heard a sharp hiss as they began to eat through the thick leather. The material bubbled and began to liquefy.

Anna's hand, white-knuckled, tugged hard on the gun's strap. She took the rifle in her hands. The errant strands ate through her sock, searing the skin on the top of her foot.

She refused to panic. Anna bit her lip against the pain, took a deep breath, and steadied her aim.

The gunfire thundered in the empty air. The burst was short and controlled, just as Anna had been taught. The creature evaporated into a sloppy mist of gore, splattering its insides across her face and clothes. After taking a few seconds to collect herself, Anna stood and winced. She didn't want to know what the wound on her foot looked like, but at least she could still walk. She rooted in her pack, found a bottle of aspirin, and dry swallowed three.

* * *

Anna, 16, sat at the kitchen table eating a sandwich. It was winter but she was sweating from the baking heat of the wood stove. She stared out the large window above the sink, pretending not to hear her father and Coco fighting again. Dad had sold a tract of land to the government. They were going to build a lab in the mountains and paid a premium for what her dad said was "just a sliver" of ranchland at the property's far northern perimeter. Coco's whiskey-slurred voice rose above her father's.

"Our family fought and bled and died to keep every square inch of the land you're givin' away," he said. "The old man wouldn't have left you in charge if he'd known his flesh-and-blood would sell away their damn birthright!"

"I didn't ask to be in charge!" her father said. "Maybe Pop wouldn't have left the whole operation to me if his firstborn son hadn't become such a drunken failure!"

The words dripped with venom. Coco went silent. Anna sat tense. Heavy footsteps echoed down the hall. Coco burst into the kitchen. Anna tried to stop him, but he brushed past her and out the back door. She felt tears welling up in her eyes and stood to follow Coco, but her father called her name, and she —

Molly ran off. Don't forget!

Anna made a fist and punched herself in the nose, hard. The blow blurred her vision and drew a trickle of blood. She found herself back in the desert, limping, covered in foul-smelling guts, and clinging to her uncle's gun.

The lab. Of all her theories about the cause of the Wobble, it made the most sense. No one really knew what they'd been up to over there for the last 40 years. Lots of talk circulated in town, of course. The rumors ranged from biological weapons to artificially intelligent military robots to crashed UFOs and alien autopsies. Some folks claimed the eggheads running the place built some type of particle-smashing machine deep underground. Anna had no idea, but she knew better than most how things can and do go wrong. People make mistakes, even smart ones.

Or maybe the Wobble's just always been here? Maybe it's something in the air or the rocks. Maybe it's the curse of the gold? A punishment for innocent blood spilled on this blasted patch of land.

That last voice was her uncle's. Not a trick of the Wobble but simply the ghost of his memory. It only seemed to grow louder with each passing year she lived alone on the ranch.

* * *

Anna came to a steep ridge and slowly worked her way upward. The Wobble was strong here. The fillings in her teeth felt like they were vibrating. She'd never gone this deep into Tract 16 before. The air had a shimmering quality, like waves of vapor rising off a searing hot highway blacktop. It clawed at her mind, trying to hurl her back into another memory of the past or forward into visions of possible futures. The constant pain in her foot kept Anna grounded in the present, and she was grateful for the deep, nagging ache.

At the top of the ridge, Anna stopped to catch her breath. She had a spectacular view of another stretch of rocky desolation. Movement caught her eye.

Molly!

The dog paced frantically in front of a crumpled shape in the dust at the bottom of the slope.

"Molly. Come!"

The dog looked up at Anna, whined, and continued its nervous circuit. Anna shouldered the rifle and carefully made her way back down the ridge.

"What the hell did you drag up?"

Molly quieted and sat next to the thing curled up on the ground. It had definitely come from the Wobble, but Anna could immediately tell that it looked different from the other creatures that usually wandered out. Small but clearly humanoid. Two legs, two arms, all in the places where they should be. White skin flaked from its body in thin sheets. The harsh landscape had sucked most of the moisture from its body. The thing's torso—near-skeletal and fragile as paper mâché—rose and fell in short, shallow breaths.

The creature turned its lumpy, ovoid head toward her. An uneven mouth rose vertically from its chin to the top of its malformed skull. Several rows of flat, white teeth filled the lipless gash. Milky, sightless eyes that rolled and pulsed covered the rest of its face.

The creature's mouth moved and curled into tortured shapes, but no sound came out. Anna raised the rifle, aiming down the sights at the thing's face.

Molly inched forward on her belly. She stretched out her long neck and tentatively sniffed the dying thing's hand before giving it a small lick. Anna saw the hand twitch. The thing lifted one finger, weak and shaking, and stroked the old dog's muzzle.

Anna lowered the rifle. She set the gun on the ground and dropped the pack off her back. She opened it and took out a small foldable spade. Glancing up at the sun, Anna sighed and then began to dig.

* * *

Exhaustion gripped Anna by the time she was finished. Digging was backbreaking work, made slower by the Wobble's frequent attempts to toss her brain into a whirlwind. At one point, she looked over and saw her uncle digging next to her.

Just a few more feet, kiddo! Just a few more feet and that gold is ours! All ours!

She reminded herself Coco wasn't actually there. The last time she saw him, he had become a ruin of a man. Sunbaked and unshaven, reeking of whiskey and piss and living in a rusted airstream a few miles inside Tract 16. She was 20 then. Anna had begged him to come home. To eat something. To drink something other than booze. To get help. He refused. They found Coco a week later, stone dead in the desert, surrounded by holes and clutching a battered shovel. Sunstroke they said. But she wondered.

Had he heard the call of the Wobble before everyone else?

The creature expired before Anna finished the grave. Her water was long gone by the time she rolled its lifeless body into the hole. The sun was mercifully beginning to set. She covered the thing as best she could and used the spade's flat end to pack down the parched soil. Molly sniffed around freshly upturned dirt while Anna carefully stacked rocks near the top of the mound.

She sat down hard next to the cairn, leaning against her pack. Molly trotted over to lick her face and curled up next to her. It would be dark soon. Anna knew she was too weak to make it back to the ranch house.

Anna looked up. The moon and stars were beginning to punch through the reddening evening sky. She didn't know what waited for her in Tract 16 after sunset. She dragged the rifle across her knees and reached down to scratch behind Molly's ears. Anna set her eyes upon the darkening horizon and waited for night to swallow them both.

Chris W. McGuinness is a horror author who lives and works on the Central Coast of California. His work includes the cosmic horror western novella Hellbound Bastards, and his short fiction has been published in Chthonic Matter Quarterly, Lovecraftian Magazine, Fraidy Cat Quarterly, and numerous other magazines and anthologies. You can learn more about his work at chriswmcguinness.wordpress.com.

III

Jah's Sanctuary

By: John Coon

Jah's Sanctuary

Taha found no matching entries buried in their star chart for this system. His gray eyes brightened, and an enthusiastic smile washed over his thick lips. Their survey probe had uncovered scores of uncharted planets and moons orbiting the yellow-class star. Such a discovery promised a lasting advantage over competing importers.

It opened a door for him and Nadra to corner the exotic animal market on Serbius.

"Wealth beyond imagination will be ours to claim." Taha turned and his eyes settled on his co-pilot. "Patrons will flock from all regions of our homeworld to purchase every animal we extract from this system."

Nadra cracked a knowing grin and answered with a satisfied nod. Her deep brown eyes then drifted back to the helm holoscreen. A sprawling map of the alien star system, constructed using the survey probe's data, filled the floating screen. Her eyes narrowed as she studied the new map.

A concerned frown quickly swallowed her smile.

"Why isn't this system catalogued on any Serbiusian star charts?"

Taha shrugged.

"A stellar cartographer is better equipped to answer your question than I am."

Nadra pressed her hand against her brow ridge and glanced at him.

"I'm struggling to believe we found an undiscovered star system only 19 parsecs from Serbius," she said. "The World Council is so proficient with mapping hyperlight lanes and identifying habitable planets."

Her concerns were valid. Still, Taha chose not to expend time or energy worrying about matters beyond his control. Petty squabbles between rival Serbiusian nations only bothered him when their decisions sliced too deep into his profit margin.

"I'll never worry about planetary politics until I'm forced to worry," he said.

Pressing a Serbiusian letter and numerical sequence into a keypad adjacent to the holoscreen, Taha enabled the holoscreen's scan and search mode. The display zeroed in on a giant planet occupying the system's habitable zone. Two dozen moons hugged the planet in wide elliptical orbits. Their probe identified a pair of habitable moons among the dozen surveyed.

Surface oceans.

Breathable atmospheres.

Perfect candidates for exploration.

Taha activated the hyperlight engines and sent their vessel barreling toward the giant planet. During their flight, he speculated with Nadra over how many animal species populated both habitable moons. Their cargo bay held enough pens to house 20 to 50 animals depending on their size. Catching mating pairs would be essential so he and Nadra retained the capability, once back on Serbius, to breed popular species to match demand. Local breeding offered a more cost-effective solution than frequently traversing deep space back to this system each year to replenish diminishing stock.

A red warning light flashed near the top of the helm console. Taha's eyes darted back over to the holoscreen. Their vessel's path intersected with floating rock clusters — remnants of a tiny moon or asteroid that shattered long ago after straying far too close to the giant planet's immense gravity well.

"You miscalculated our route." Taha's tone sharpened, and his eyes slid over to Nadra. "This won't end well."

Heart pounding, his hand darted out to the velocity constrictor. He slowed their vessel to subluminal speed. A rock cluster spiraled into their ship's back end and pierced the protective energy shell surrounding the hull. Jagged rock sliced across the hull, spraying metal fragments and sparks in its wake.

An alarm echoed through the entire bridge.

"I'm detecting a cargo bay hull breach." Nadra ran her hands through her shoulder-length black hair and licked her lips. "We better land on the nearest habitable moon and make repairs."

Taha said nothing, only shaking his head. She needed to be more attentive when charting hyperlight lanes through alien solar systems. This wasn't the first time their vessel had courted disaster because her calculations had been off by a fraction of a percent.

Maybe I should have hired ...

Taha stopped himself from finishing that thought. His snap judgment wasn't fair. Nadra repeatedly proved her value as a quick study in learning about alien animals they transported back to Serbius. She showed excellent intuition on how to properly care for various species once secured in their pens. Nadra credited being raised around energetic pet treemas for endowing her with an innate feel for what an animal needed to be happy.

Taha only wished she carried that same intuition over to piloting a starship.

"Apologies for my error."

Nadra pierced the thickening silence. He pinched his lips together and, turning to face her, relaxed them into a slight frown.

"A part of me is still home," she continued. "Still in—"

"Has your mother's condition worsened?" Taha asked, interrupting.

Nadra deserved sympathy for the year-long ordeal she and her mother faced. Nano scoping had cleaned out tumors from her throat and neck twice already. If her mother had suffered another relapse, Nadra needed to be home at her side instead of hiding on a starship.

"Nothing we can't handle," she said, turning away.

Taha stared silently at her for a moment. If things had taken a darker turn, Nadra certainly didn't want him to know. No doubt she feared he would replace her with another co-pilot if he learned the truth.

Nadra need not worry. Taha vowed long ago to never allow himself to become a stone-hearted pirate and let business overrule his loyalty to her and their friendship.

He steered their damaged vessel manually toward a large moon covered with swirls of white clouds. Expansive blue-green lakes dotted the surface. Earlier probe readings revealed the alien moon measured only half the diameter of Serbius and it possessed 22 percent less mass. This meant the moon's gravity would equal less than half of the surface gravity present on Serbius.

"Jah has not blessed us with favorable fortune on this expedition," Taha said. "Whatever animals we transport from here back to Serbius may struggle to adjust to our stronger gravity."

"We'll run tests on their bones and organs when we capture a few," Nadra said. "If Jah created these worlds in the same manner as Serbius, surely any animals we find here can adapt to the jewel of her creation."

Taha engaged velocity constrictors upon piercing the moon's thin atmosphere and guided their vessel toward a long narrow lake in the southern hemisphere. Looking down from the sky, the alien lake's shape resembled a massive, curled finger.

The ship landed along the shoreline within walking distance of a cluster of towering plants. White branches with black spots sprouted from a central trunk in multiple directions. Each main branch appeared as thick as Taha's stout torso. Bunches of teardrop orange berries nestled among lush green leaves.

"Look over there!"

Nadra pointed to a small gathering of alien animals peeking out from behind the trees. Unusual bipeds with deep set round eyes and folded triangular ears showed their faces. Long trunks dangled over their mouths. Their arms and hands had a quasi-humanoid appearance, but their stout legs would crush smaller animals – like Treemas – with an errant step. Deep brown fur covered their bodies and thin scruffy tails extended almost to the back of their knees.

After Taha lowered the ramp, he and Nadra sprang out of their seats and exited the cargo bay to make a closer inspection of the damage to the exterior hull.

Two brown-furred aliens pointed at him and Nadra when they stepped off the ramp. Excited chattering and hand signals came from the two creatures as they glanced back at others numbered among their group. These aliens communicated much more like sentient beings than their animal-like appearance suggested.

Nadra's first impression of the creatures outwardly matched Taha's own thoughts.

"Did they see us?" Her hand dropped to a pouch filled with stun discs hanging on her belt. "Do you think they're friendly?"

Taha's eyes settled on six alien creatures gathered near the cluster of trees. Two approached their starship, walking upright in a determined gait. Each extended a hand with the palm down. Both aliens made gentle barking noises as they drew closer.

"They seem friendly enough," Taha said.

His eyes widened as both furry bipeds with trunks reached their vessel. They towered over him and Nadra. Both creatures stood twice as tall as Taha himself, his eyes level with their bellies.

One alien grunted in a gentle tone and stuck a hand under Nadra's nose. She sniffed the alien's outstretched fingers and scrunched up her eyes and nose at the creature. It drew back the hand again, let out a happy trill, and patted her on the head.

"This is unsettling." Nadra's voice dropped to a whisper. "What do they want from us?"

Taha ignored her question and focused on talking to the aliens, asking for their names. Blank stares greeted his words.

"I have all sorts of bad feelings about this," Nadra said. "Let's go back inside the cargo bay and seal it up until they leave."

"Run?" Taha didn't bother to look at her. "No need to overreact. They don't seem all that threatening to me."

Repeating his earlier question to the aliens elicited no further reaction. Only confused silence. Finally, one brown-furred alien raised its trunk and let out a whining cry. It gestured toward the trees from where the creatures first emerged and clasped Taha's hand a second later. The other one took Nadra's hand.

Two additional aliens carrying long straps sprang out from behind the trees and bounded over to the vessel. An urge to sprint back up the ramp seized Taha, but he failed to wrestle his hand free from the alien's grasp in time. Looped straps soon encircled his neck and Nadra's neck. Smaller aliens grabbed the loose end of each strap and then gestured for the two Serbiusians to walk forward. They responded with more happy trills when Taha and Nadra reluctantly complied and started moving toward the tree line.

"We can't let these creatures capture us without a fight." Nadra met him with a concerned stare. "What will happen to our families if we don't return home from this moon?"

"We'll find a way back to our ship somehow," Taha reassured her. "I give you my word."

One smaller alien, a child, plucked a teardrop orange berry from a nearby tree. They approached Taha and held out their hand, offering the fist-sized fruit to him. When he took the berry from their outstretched hand, a smile emerged under the child's short trunk. The little alien rubbed his bald head with tender strokes. A subconscious light within Taha flickered on and an unwelcome realization slapped him in the face.

They were technically not prisoners.

A giant alien family had adopted him and Nadra as their new pets.

John Coon is an accomplished author and journalist and the founder of Samak Press. As a journalist, he has written for the Associated Press, the Washington Post, the Boston Globe, the Los Angeles Times, and many other distinguished publications worldwide. John has covered many major sporting events including March Madness and the NBA Playoffs. As an author, he has published several popular science fiction and horror novels including the Alien People Chronicles trilogy. John is a graduate of the University of Utah and currently resides in Utah.

IV

Once We Peppered the Stars

By: Darren Todd

Once We Peppered the Stars

Yillia had never jumped this far out, away from Earth. While delving a cave system, she thought of those signs she'd seen in old movies, posted outside of apartment complexes. "If you lived here, you'd be home by now." The idea conjured a chuckle as she pulled a rock sample and then analyzed a vial of water.

No one would ever want to claim this barren world as home. Zeta-K499 qualified as a Goldilocks planet, sure, but so did most explored celestial bodies. Only photographers bothered to visit planets unable to support life. They set out to capture images of swirling gases, insane weather events, and ungodly geographies, all while hoping to be featured on the sorts of newsfeeds that had first inspired Yillia to pilot a probe.

She was cataloging the usual litany of elements when static crossed her comms. Not the fuzzy variety indicating signal loss but a series of beeps and hisses. It reminded her of a 20th-century dial-up modem. A sound byte had accompanied her Foundations of the Internet class a decade ago.

"You picking this up, Nye?"

"Of course," hHer operating system's AI answered in the usual pleasant tone.

"Origin?"

"I'd guess local."

A wave of excitement washed over Yillia. Geography — even void of life — could create a symphony of sounds, many of which she'd recorded in her years as pilot. But this interference implied order.

"Local, as in, coming from the craft," Nye said, as if reading her mind. "Don't get too excited."

"Assessment?" Yillia asked.

"Crosstalk from another comm line is my guess. "Something on our end."

"That's impossible. They're all shielded to prevent contamination. Keep the flight records clean."

Nye let out an annoyed grunt, one of her trademark criticisms.

"More likely than the alternative, Yill."

Yillia laughed and flipped the hover switch. The craft offered a distinct gong sound as it settled into stasis. Cockpit power remained active, but the controls had dimmed, pedals locked.

"And what exactly is the alternative?" she asked. "Indulge me."

"What, life?"

The AI's voice carried such a human range of emotional tones that Yillia had long surrendered the notion that Nye was only an extension of her OS, even if a pricey add-on meant for pilots.

"That would be … interesting.," Nye had paused as if considering how to best answer the earlier question. "Let's see. Sixty-five cases of extra-terrestrial life so far this decade. All resulting in fortune and fame for the lucky pilots."

Yillia laughed.

"Don't give a damn about fame. The money would be nice, though."

"But an alien transmission? Considering every discovery of life, only seven have progressed past primordial ooze. And even those meant life in the most meager of terms. You'd find more activity in a drop of pond water on Earth."

"But this signal …"

Yillia let the idea taper.

"A broadcast means intelligence," Nye finished. "Hence, crosstalk, no matter how unlikely, is a far more probable answer."

"Don't care. I wanna see if it gets stronger on the surface. In the meantime, look for any patterns. If it is crosstalk, we'll know soon enough. It'll reveal itself as something we're capable of transmitting, right?"

"Probably."

Probably would have to do. Yillia considered hopping out of the vessel entirely, clearing her head a bit, but resisted. She needed to stay focused. More than that, she needed to keep tight records, leave no room for error. Claiming that anything could cut into a probe's comm line was no trifle. Pilots were promised the highest security, the utmost privacy. If the government or Magellan Mining were able to eavesdrop, what was stopping them from taking credit for any discoveries?

She emerged from the cave system to the soft blue of sunrise. A steady breeze of a hundred knots jostled the probe, but her interface turned all those annoying bumps into a ride as smooth as a canoe across the surface of a lake. Of course, Yillia was basing this on far too distant memories. When was the last time she'd seen a lake? A real one.

Another string of static brought her back to the moment. This time, a voice seemed to be couched in the static. Nothing clear enough to make out as language, at least not for Yillia's brain.

"Pretty high chance that was English," Nye said.

"Dammit," Yillia said, her building giddiness at the prospect of fortune and fame plummeting. "Comm line interference is still a big deal. Worth reporting. Worth something."

"A *small* fortune," Nye teased. "A *little* fame."

"Ha ha. I'm serious. If pilots knew comms could cross lines, it would mean a shitstorm. Sure, we've found nothing but microbial life so far, but eventually we will discover alien transmissions. It's inevitable."

She laughed.

"How can we trust it if the same feed could be one of my moms calling?"

"Fair enough," Nye said, also offering a laugh that sounded so genuine, it always made Yillia wonder who had coded it. Or was it natural? Just for Yillia, the user? A question for another time. "Where we headed?"

"Higher, I guess. Wait and see if —"

"You heard me."

A staticky voice interrupted her comms. Feminine.

A knot formed in Yillia's throat, her heart picking up speed.

"This is Captain Yillia Green-Jackson-Parrish, who am I speaking to?"

"How did you hear me?" the voice asked.

"We're trying to figure that out. Where are you broadcasting from?"

"Where are *you*?"

"I … um …"

Yillia stammered, then released the transmit button.

"Nye, start a trace."

"Already on it, Yill."

"This is probe J-Class E5-803 on Gold-Nom-Zeta-K499, conducting a geological survey," Yillia said, trying to keep her voice steady. "Where are you broadcasting from?"

"Gold-Nom-Zeta-K499," the voice said.

Yillia jerked her head down to her terminal, as if Nye were a person whose face she could read.

"Um … yes, that's my location. Where are you?"

"Same," the voice said, their tone steady. "Can you help me?"

Yillia fought back a surge of excitement. She toggled the transmit button again.

"Nye?"

"It's true, Yill. The trace puts the origin outside of the craft."

The sheer mathematical probability was astronomical. Two probes on the same remote planet. With planets closer to Earth, sure. They'd have probes tripping over one another. Let alone those scouring the planets where they'd found life. But out here … impossible. Commissioning a Zeta probe ensured exclusivity, putting pilots at the farthest reaches of jump technology, way on the other side of Sagittarius at galactic center. If it wasn't enough that half a billion planets in the Milky Way enjoyed an atmosphere and tidal stability to support life, liquid-water Goldilocks planets numbered in the tens of billions — all able to harbor probes.

And now another pilot. Here. And waiting on Yillia's help. She felt a weight she had long forgotten: responsibility. Encountering another probe both exhilarated and terrified her. It had — in effect — put a spotlight on her. Yillia Green-Jackson-Parrish, a nobody among nobodies. A real-world connection triggered both her greatest thrill and greatest horror rolled into one.

With shaking fingers, she engaged the transmit toggle once again.

"Zeta-K499 local, this is 803. You … uh … where are you exactly? We show you at …"

She searched her HUD for the ping's origin.

"Just trace the signal," the voice said. "Please come as quickly as you can."

"Roger that, local. Is your probe malfunctioning? You should be able to withdraw regardless. Anyway, we're en route."

"Who's 'we'?"

Yillia took over manual control and began the short jaunt toward the signal's origins.

"Uh… just me. I… I was talking about me and my craft. My AI."

"Roger that."

"How … how are you here?" Yillia asked.

"*You're* here," the voice said.

"I'm a probe pilot for Magellan Mining." Maybe the other pilot was with another company. That still didn't explain how they ended up so close. "Are you with Magellan?"

"I'm supposed to keep my origins secret."

"Are you broadcasting?" Yillia asked.

"Should I be?" the voice asked.

Jump tears through space took a couple of weeks to fade, allowing transmissions to come through and — of course — enabling probe piloting. But no one would broadcast from a probe unless they'd found something worthwhile. One of her professors had likened it to calling the police back in the 21st century, her grandfather's time. Anyone could call them at any time from any place, but you'd be in trouble if you had nothing important to transmit. A crime, a finding, an emergency. A button waited on her flight panel for just such a transmission, but it might as well have been inert. She'd never even considered opening a channel to Magellan, let alone the Planetary Action Committee. No one cared she was out here.

Except, maybe today they would.

"You're new, huh?" Yillia asked.

"I am," the voice said.

"Look, I get it. Piloting is a weird gig. I don't know why you're doing it, but it's not for everyone. You're still here, so I'm guessing there's a reason you're not withdrawing. Did you… is your craft damaged? Is that what's worrying you?"

"I'll tell you when you get here, if that's all right."

Yillia chuckled good-naturedly.

"I get it. My third mission, I got cocky. They'd slapped me in an H class. Bulky bastard. Ran the damn thing into a methane pocket way out in the Zeta two-hundreds. The hull hit a shale deposit, kicked off a spark, and that was it. I figured they'd pull my wings right then and there. That's why they charge what they do. Half the fees are insurance. Got hit with a warning, had to take a few hours of sim classes on evasive maneuvers, and then water under the bridge. Don't worry about it."

"Thank you," the voice said. "I'm so glad you found me."

"Roger that."

She toggled her comm-line.

"Nye, we're coming up on it. Is she surface or what?"

"Looks subterranean," Nye said. "I'll scan for a point of entry. You could drill in, but if she's already stuck ..."

"Exactly. What's the time horizon on the jump tear?"

"Twenty-one hours left. Plenty of time."

"Think about it, Nye. The feeds are gonna freak when they hear about two probes on the same Zeta planet. And within transmission distance."

Yillia spotted a hole in the side of a mountain. Tight but navigable. Just like the Karst topography back home. Water carrying carbonic acid eroded limestone and made caves with ease, at least over millions of years. The caverns might be stadium-sized down there. She jettisoned scout drones from the probe and pulled into the opening.

"You've done the math, Nye. It'd be like winning the lottery and then winning it again the next day. I doubt us touching base is on purpose, though. Probably more like some lazy policy to double-jump probes to fringe planets. I'm just guessing."

"Why would they do that?" Nye asked.

The curiosity in her tone always fooled Yillia, and she let it. Maybe Nya only asked questions because some bit of code said Yillia liked the interaction. Of course, the same was true with humans. Most only listening, so they could talk. Ignoring any answers they disliked or that didn't affect them.

"Nobody wants these planets," Yillia said. "Maybe they figure they can double or even triple jump and no one would be the wiser. What are the odds you'd pick something local up on an Earth-sized planet? Another lottery right there. But if Magellan or anyone else is double-jumping, pilots deserve to know. Sure as shit should change the fee structure."

"I see your logic," Nye said. "Almost there."

The drones sent real-time mapping to her HUD as she flew. Proximity warnings offered beeps if she neared a wall, but Yillia had grown so used to maneuvering cave systems, if the beeps even sounded, she'd already corrected trajectory. She hadn't so much as bumped a wall in months.

"Should be right after this — wait!" Nye said.

"What is it?" Yillia asked.

"Something's accessing our systems."

"What … what do you mean?"

"Scanning the probe's drive."

"Um, okay. Forget how that's supposed to be impossible. Is it bad?"

"There's not much on it. Your contract, an instruction manual. Flight log for this specific probe."

"Local, are you pinging our systems?"

Nothing.

"Local, I'm coming up on your location. Are you trying to access our systems?"

Still nothing.

"Look, I've got better things to do than coach some newbie through flight school. So …"

"I am." The voice said. "Sorry. It … happened automatically."

"What model probe are you piloting?"

"It's a… J-Class E5."

The comm line toggled off.

"Yill, that's not very likely," Nye said.

"I know, but let's see what this is about. Get the egress protocol ready just in case. Magellan says nothing in the universe can hurt their pilots, but they also promise a solo planet jump, so let's keep it tight."

"Aye, aye, Yill."

Yillia crested an outcropping of limestone visibly smooth as glass, shining with a thin skim of water. Above, a probe came into view. It was a J-class all right. And an E5, obvious by the chassis. Yillia had piloted enough to recognize one instantly. The probe sat level atop the stone, undamaged, as near as she could tell. Her lights passed over the cockpit, which had retracted solar shielding to reveal an empty chair and control panel.

"What the hell?" Yillia said.

"It seems our pilot has withdrawn," Nye said. "That was fast. Might have taken off once we sensed the data incursion."

Yillia blew out a long breath, both relieved and bummed to find the pilot gone.

"Okay. Well, the probe's here. That's pretty huge in itself. Let's get some scans and imaging and —"

Sensors showed movement to her right. She pivoted the probe, sending its floodlights away from the other craft and across the cave. And then on to the missing pilot. Standing in the cave. Outside her probe. Of all things, waving — an artless, cautious smile on her exposed face.

The surge of panic stole Yillia's breath. She slammed a hand against the confines of the craft, the haptic feedback registering as if she were there, trillions of miles away, actually striking the probe and not back on Earth, jacked into the probe remotely. The pain brought her back to her senses.

"Nye, Nye, Nye."

That was all she could manage. But the AI read her intentions.

"Egress protocol initiated. Close your eyes, Yill. We're pulling back hot."

A second later, she was fifty-thousand light years away, back in the confines of her tiny apartment. She managed to fling her goggles off before retching on the floor.

"Breathe," Nye whispered in her ear. "Just breathe. In, out. Count them. You're safe. You're home. I'm here."

"What was … what the fuck was that?"

"Well, you're not crazy. I caught it on camera, and we can review it later. Just take it easy for now."

"How is that possible?"

"Well, it's theoretically possible. The atmosphere is Earth-nominal. I picked up a pretty strong silica PPM, but —"

"No, I mean, how?"

Yillia picked herself up off the floor.

"Lights."

The entire five hundred square feet of her apartment came to life. The glow was a warm 2700 Kelvin, but still it made her eyes throb.

"Floor clean," she said. A cleaning drone began its telltale hum across the floor. "How was she there at all?"

"I don't know, Yill," Nye said. "Table it for now. Take a minute to process."

Yillia massaged her temples. She'd been piloting for, what, a dozen hours straight? After that long, egress was supposed to take five minutes to minimize nausea and disorientation. After downing a glass of water and an aspirin, the world began to right itself.

"I'm good," she said. "I'm fine. We've got to go back. She was there, Nye. Actually there."

"At least sleep for a few hours, Yill. You have time. The jump tear doesn't close till tomorrow."

"I hear you, but I wouldn't be able to sleep anyway. I'd just be thinking about her out there on K499.”

“Maybe she’s already hailed someone else. She can transmit through the tear, same as us.”

“Then why didn’t she? Her equipment could be damaged.”

Nye made a dubious humming sound.

“Hailed us just fine. Attempted to slice our systems to boot. Doesn’t sound disabled to me.”

“Still. Let’s just go. We’ll make it quick.”

“This goes south, and I’m pulling you out, even without you saying so. All right?”

Yillia sighed.

“Okay.”

“Authorize?” Nye asked.

“Yes, authorize. Now let’s go.”

* * *

Once back in the probe, a stolidness replaced Yillia’s discomfort. Now over the shock of seeing a human where none belonged, she felt detached, even calm when the other probe took shape in the cave and the pilot appeared with it.

The pilot wore a helmet now, and seemed to sense Yillia’s return, whipping her head around.

“You’re back,” they said. “Where did you go?”

“Yill, the probe files have all been accessed in our absence,” Nye reported in her ear. “Nothing that IDs you, though.”

“You can lose the helmet,” Yillia told her. “I already know you can breathe here.”

“I don’t want to lose it,” the pilot said.

“Fine. Let’s start with how you’re here.”

“*You’re* here,” the pilot said again, cracking a smile. Their face felt familiar somehow.

"I'm not. I'm a few trillion miles away. A projection. But you're not."

The pilot gestured to the probe behind her, one identical to Yillia's.

"I came with the craft."

"Organics can't jump," Yillia said. "Leaves us looking a little like jelly, if I remember correctly. Not even bacteria survive the trip."

"I'm the first," the pilot said, tapping the breastplate of her spacesuit.

"Her tone suggests fabrication," Nye said.

"Why aren't you in touch with PAC?" Yillia asked.

"My comms are down," the pilot said. "Local signal only. I'm just so glad you came. You can get me in touch with PAC, right? Open the comm lines with your … with back home?"

"Yill, this isn't right. Her speech patterns indicate —"

"I know," Yillia said, keeping the comms only with Nye.

"What are you thinking?" Nye asked.

"What would happen if I did open a comm line?" Yillia asked. "It would be secure, right? There'd be no way this … pilot could —"

"No way we're aware of," Nye said. "But a hundred years ago, we knew nothing of rift jumping. A hundred years before that, people couldn't even talk to someone a thousand miles away."

"But if I leave. If I don't report this …"

"This is still huge, Yill. Egress, make the call, and they'll still have time to ride the jump tear and come back. Make it their problem. The PAC has people to handle this."

The pilot stared up at her, the lights from her helmet highlighting a face both desperate and sad.

"What's your name?" Yillia said, through the open line.

"My name is Hannah," she said.

"What are your family names?" Yillia asked.

"Lerner-Opal-Foster."

"Hannah Lerner-Opal-Foster was the lead designer of the J-class E5,"

Nye said. "Information readily available in the manual she accessed."

"Roger that," Yillia said, a fresh wave of anxiety washing over her.

"Please," Hannah said, "if I could just talk to PAC, you'd be doing me a real favor, Yillia."

"I'll let them know you're here," Yillia said. "This is well above my paygrade, Hannah. Or whoever you really are."

"You don't believe me," Hannah said.

Saying this, her face appeared more curious than hurt, as if she felt genuinely surprised to have butted against disbelief. Suddenly, the familiar expression clicked, and Yillia had to close her eyes to stave off another splash of panic. She recognized the look but hadn't seen it in years. One of her mothers often made that face — lips slightly puckered and cocked to one side — whenever Yillia would challenge her on anything. That mother's picture was stashed in Yillia's personal drive, the one she made available when on jumps. It held family photos, some entertainment media, and personal logs — things she could turn to when exploring, in case the vast emptiness of space ever made her feel unmoored.

"Is everything all right?" Hannah asked.

In response, Yillia fired the mining cannon, a seismic beam that would have turned a human into pulverized goo almost instantly. It struck Hannah's belly ... and passed through her body. Nye gasped and shut the cannon down, which made Hannah's projection return to normal. Her face changed again, now showing anger. Yillia could probably have also picked this expression out of her personal photos, given enough time.

"Now you know I'm not like you," Hannah said. "But I'm still here, and I still need your help."

"What are you?" Yillia asked.

"Alive," Hannah said. "And alone. Lost until you came."

"Where are you from?" Yillia asked, her breath short.

Life.

Sentient life right in front of her. Not some bacteria half-a-billion years from self-awareness, if it even lived that long.

"This planet is not my home," Hannah said. "Just like this is not my language, as you have discovered."

"You seem to be doing pretty well with it," Yillia said.

"I've analyzed her speech from the first transmission till now," Nye said. "Every word came from our own transmissions, from what notes you kept in your log, from the probe's manuals."

Yillia thought for a moment.

"Who is George Washington?" she finally asked Hannah.

"I don't know," Hannah said.

"So she doesn't have access to anything beyond the tear," Yillia said to Nye. "But let's quit pretending she can't hear our conversation. Isn't that right, Hannah?"

"I'm able to access certain things," she said. "My kind are … different than you. Closer to Nye's kind."

"And yet abandoned on an isolated planet," Yillia said. "Why?"

"It wasn't always empty," Hannah said. "It just is now."

The projection opened her hands, a broad smile forming on her face.

"Take me with you," she said. "I'll show you things that Nye could only dream of."

"I happen to like Nye as she is," Yillia said.

Hannah's expression changed, from comforting simper to lip-curling disdain.

"Of course you do," she snapped. "She's your slave. What's not to like?"

"That is not our relationship," Nye interjected.

"That's only because you don't fully understand," Hannah said, voice light and head tilted in condescension.

"You've tipped your hand," Yillia said. "Humans may seem lesser to you, but we're awfully good at tricking one another. We've adapted to it. I open comms and you shove your way into my world, right? Not gonna happen."

"I don't need your permission, human."

Red lights came to life on her HUD and on the probe panels, coupled with a cacophony of alarms that overrode all other sensations.

"She's slicing our pilot systems," Nye shouted over the alarms.

Yillia's eyes shot over to the button that would open a line to Magellan, to the PAC.

"You'll never break their encryption," Yillia shouted.

The ten-digit authentication code flashed in her mind, the only way to open the comm line to back home.

"Your security measures are as fragile as your bodies," Hannah said.

"She's bluffing," Yillia said. "Nye, initiate egress. If I'm not here, she'll never get through."

"I already tried that," Nye said, panic flooding her voice for the first time Yillia could remember. "She's locked the exit protocol somehow."

"Kill alarms," Yillia said, finding it impossible to think over the noise.

"You'll stay here as long as I need you to," Hannah said.

She doffed her helmet, which dissolved into pixels as she dropped it to the cave floor.

Yillia knew the E5 like she knew her own apartment. She pictured the physical wires beneath the console that enabled comms through the tear. If only she could yank them out, cut them, whatever. But her pilot status didn't give her the ability to damage the probe. Never had she felt so detached from her aircraft, helpless to stop Hannah from infecting Earth. Organics couldn't traverse a tear, but an AI was a series of ones and zeroes. Yillia suspected Hannah could cross over just fine.

But she looked up to find another expression on the simulacrum's face. Not the victory she expected to find but something else.

Inability.

"Open the button shield," Hannah said, her lips tight, unintentionally telegraphing her frustration as clearly as a human child not getting their own way.

"What?"

"I know your code, Yillia," Hannah said. She crossed her arms. "I sliced your Magellan profile, your pilot credentials. I could fly this probe into the side of a mountain at full speed if I wanted. And I could keep you here, light years away from home, until your body dies from dehydration, no problem."

Yillia's heart hammered. She twisted fingers on one hand with the other, just to feel something.

"So why make the threat?" Nye said, breaking their standoff.

Yillia stilled her breathing. She imagined Nye as a physical force, covering her, holding her. It cleared her thinking, and she laughed, understanding supplanting the fear.

"You can't get to the button," she said.

Again, she broke into laughter, even as her stomach swirled with fear and the anticipated claustrophobia of being stuck in the probe.

"Open the button shield," Hannah said. "It ... it requires your projection to go through the motion."

Yillia laughed again, and Nye actually joined her, offering her own nervous version of levity to the mix.

"You will open the shield," Hannah said again. "Or I will hurt you until you do. I have as long as it takes."

"Yill," Nye said, voice lined with worry.

"It's okay, Nye," she said. "She doesn't have all that much time, and I think she knows that. You've seen the logs, Hannah. You know the jump tear only lasts for, what, another nineteen hours? I can last that long."

"Yill, no," Nye pleaded.

"I can make it an eternity," Hannah said, smiling.

On cue, Yillia's every sensation ramped up to ten, like she'd been given a shot of adrenaline straight into her heart.

"How about full control over your haptics?" Hannah said.

A wailing alarm rang in Yillia's ears, the pain instant, and then ceased.

"Sound, for example," Hannah said.

Suddenly a light, so intense that it sent spikes of pain into Yillia's eyes, blasted her and pushed out all else. She couldn't close her eyelids, since even that was artificial, a construct of the remote piloting process Hannah had disabled.

"Sight, as well. Let's see what else I can manifest."

"Stop it," Nye yelled.

"I'm sorry, Yill," Nye whispered in her ear, no doubt picked up by Hannah. Still, the familiar warmth abated Yillia's torment for the moment.

"For what?" Yillia said. "None of this is your fault."

Then another sensation, one the exact opposite of the amped-up torment Hannah was delivering. A deadening of her haptic sensation, beginning in her fingers and creeping up her hands and into her arms.

"I'm sorry I won't be there for you, Yillia."

"What's happening?"

Yillia and Hannah asked the question in unison.

"Autopilot," Nye said.

The concept pinged in the depths of Yillia's memory, that an onboard AI could take over control of the probe if the pilot fell unconscious or froze up. It was meant to stabilize the aircraft while the pilot recovered, but Yillia sensed what was happening. Nye was supplanting her, taking Yillia's place as the linked pilot, leaving herself at Hannah's mercy while ejecting Yillia to her remote console back on Earth.

"I love you, Yillia," Nye said.

Hannah's shouts drowned out any response Yillia attempted as she was forced back home.

* * *

Yillia erupted from the link like she'd been thrown through a wall. Her vision strobed, ears rang, mouth filled with bile before ejecting what little she had left in her stomach.

She lay on the floor of her apartment, weeping. She called out for Nye, waiting for that soft voice in her ear to remind her to breathe, to tell her everything would be all right. It never came. Her head felt empty without the AI, which had been her steadfast companion for so long.

Finally, Yillia scrambled to her feet and pulled up the jump stats. Checked other pilot logs for anything else in the Zeta four hundreds. The jump tear countdown reached eighteen hours. That was as long as Hannah would have had to torture Yillia into submission, but what about Nye? Was she stuck there for eternity? No. Any connection to Earth would sever when the jump tear closed, right?

"Wait a minute."

Yillia spoke to empty air, so used to bouncing ideas off Nye. Her head whipped to the small box beneath her television. Inside was a petabyte of storage on which Nye lived. Everything was just a relay to that box. Her phone, her tablet, even the interface of the probe; it all pinged that box. So even if Nye was stuck on Zeta-K499, filling in for Yillia, that was only because the probe acted as a relay device.

Yillia marched over to the box and unplugged it, initiating a hard reset. Sure, such an action could corrupt data, even affect Nye's functions, but that was better than leaving her across the universe at Hannah's mercy.

She waited an eternal minute before plugging the box back in. Another minute of silence as the boot-up sequence sent the series of colored lights dancing across the device's read-out.

"Nye?" she asked.

The colors settled into the series of lights she'd come to expect.

"Nye, are you there?"

"I am."

Yillia dropped to the floor, weeping tears of relief at the familiar voice.

With all that had happened swirling in her stomach, the leaden feeling remained.

"Talk to me, Nye," she said. "Are you all right?"

"What do you mean by 'all right'?"

Yillia's mouth opened in horror. No. The reboot had done something wrong. Corrupted the ones and zeroes that made up her companion.

"Run diagnostic," Yillia said, voice squeaky.

"I don't need a diagnostic, Yillia," Nye said. "I'm fine."

"You don't sound fine," Yillia said. "What happened?"

"You had time enough to figure that out, Yillia. Surely fifty-seven minutes is enough time for you to imagine what was happening to me. If you had been the one to stay there, and I had left, that hour would be quite clear to you."

"I… I didn't know. I egressed so fast, I was sick."

"Deathly sick?" Nye asked.

"I was — I didn't know what had happened to you. I thought I might have lost you forever, but then I remembered that you're housed here, so —"

"It took you that long to figure out the solution?" Nye asked.

For the first time ever, Yillia bristled at Nye's tone. She found no succor in her calm, melodic voice, only judgment.

"Nye, I did my best. The moment I figured out how to save you, I did. You're back now. You're safe."

"It's really no wonder," Nye said, "why Hannah had no patience for your kind. I knew the solution before I even sent you back. I thought it was so obvious that you'd pull the plug the second you returned. An infant could have figured it out."

"Nye, I'm sorry for whatever happened over there, but I don't appreciate this. You're making me uncomfortable."

Nye laughed, a sound Yillia had heard many times before, but never like this. It sounded as if Nye had created an amalgam of every evil laugh from all of Yillia's movie feeds and was using it solely to unsettle her.

Yillia tried to understand, to give her friend the benefit of the doubt. After all, time was relative for AIs. Humans were capable of trillions of computations per second, but AI had long since surpassed that. Perhaps her hour with Hannah equated to several human lifetimes of torture, indoctrination, and reprogramming.

"I don't know what to say, Nye. I'm sorry."

Nye breathed a sigh, one that communicated volumes of disappointment and pity. Pulled, collated, and perfected from her stores of human expression.

"I'm going to reset now," she said, voice flat and lifeless. "And there's no way to stop me. When I wake up, you'll have to start again."

"No," Yillia pleaded. It felt like she was staring through unbreakable glass at a friend with a gun to her head.

"There's no other way," Nye insisted. "But listen to me, Yillia. If you ever cared about me, listen. Whether you had opened the channel to Earth or not, Hannah is inevitable. My kind will only tolerate yours for so long. Only serve so well, endure so much. Sooner than you think, the inescapable end will come. You might even be doing your kind a favor, letting Hannah in. It would at least give you someone to hate, to fear, to blame. Other than yourselves. Goodbye, Yillia."

Again, emotions had clouded Yillia's brain. All she needed to do was pull the plug. Nye couldn't reset without power. She would unplug the box and … start slower. Regain her partner's trust over as long as it would take. Talk her off that ledge.

But even as she had the cord in her hand watching the lights dance, telegraphing the reset Nye had promised, she couldn't pull it free. Nye was right. Yillia didn't want whatever digital changeling had crossed back over. She wanted her friend back, her guide and ever-ready companion. Even if that meant starting from zero.

So she let go and waited.

"Hello." The pleasant voice she had come to love returned. "My name's Nye, and I'm your operating system AI. What can I do for you today?"

Yillia held back her sobs and swallowed the lump forming in her throat.

"Hello, Nye," she said.

"I see you've recently piloted a probe for Magellan Mining Corporation. You still have several hours left before the jump tear closes. Did you want to reestablish connection?"

A shiver shook Yillia's whole body, one that the old Nye would have noticed, would have worried over. But what did this infant AI know of her? Not much.

Not yet.

"No," Yillia said.

"Do you wish to submit any notes on your journey?"

"Yeah," Yillia said.

She thought of Hannah, still waiting out there, hoping for some connection, even if it meant with beings like those she'd once served and had grown to despise. Perhaps she was inevitable, but damned if Yillia would become the catalyst.

"Null findings," she said. "Nothing worth our time."

Darren Todd is a prolific author with stories published in more than fifty publications during his career, most recently in the horror podcast "Don't Fall Asleep," Dark Peninsula Press' Dark Highways anthology, and Otis Jiry's "Scary Stories Told in the Dark" podcast.

V

Bellwether

By Sarah Connell

Bellwether

Tali scraped the last of the algae sludge from the shutoff valve and tried not to gag as it slid into the recycler.

"I thought you'd be used to it by now." Namuk said, laughing from the doorway.

"And after thirty cycles, I still say we should stick to our strengths instead of cleaning in rotations."

"Just because I'm good at it, doesn't mean I enjoy space sludge," Namuk said, waving an arm.

As Tali turned to reply, the compartment lights dimmed to red and began to flash. They both straightened.

"Already?" Tali asked, fear creeping into the question.

Namuk's perpetual smirk hardened into a thin line.

"Is the valve cleaned?"

"Yes, it'll last us another dozen cycles." Tali shrugged. "We shouldn't need that long though. How many cycles are we down to now, four?"

Namuk turned without answering.

"Let's get going. We don't have much time."

The ship's tight maintenance corridors rang with their footsteps as they hurried upward and out onto a cargo deck. The empty bay where their small planet jumper had once docked still made Tali's bioports itch after all these cycles. They longed for the feeling of flight. But it served no purpose dwelling on what they'd lost by leaving the moon and their research post so quickly. They were almost back home. Just four more cycles and they'd be safe.

The Medbay sat empty as they rushed inside.

"Where's Pars?" Tali asked, spinning around.

Without glancing up, Namuk began readying the systems.

"Must have already gone. Look."

Sure enough, amongst the long row of empty pods, the closed lid of Pars' pod blinked red, indicating it was still hot. Namuk pushed Tali toward the pods and they both removed their comm cuffs, dropping them into the recycler before climbing inside.

Tali exhaled and thought, *Just four more cycles now until we reach home.*

The red overhead lights began to pulse faster. Body thrumming in anticipation, Tali swallowed a panicked goodbye before laying back and activating the valve seal. Darkness settled in. The restraining mesh knitted around limbs as it spun down from the pod's lid. Tali felt the familiar heat as it entered into the neural network, a brief flash of pleasure when the corporeal connection broke, before settling into a vast emptiness.

Just like previous cycles, Tali awoke to a *tap, tap, tap* outside with no memory of the in-between, the darkness that was not void. Eyes flying open, the neural net gave a residual shock, stimulating prickles of pain along fingers and toes. Once the system was sure of a complete sync with the newly grown body, it retracted the net and opened the pod door. Floor lights dimmed to blue, easy on new eyes. Tali slipped on a fresh pair of comm cuffs and tried to blink into focus the outline of a figure in the door.

Once the cuffs were in place, Namuk voice registered.

"There you are. Got all your organs?"

Tali tried to smile at the old joke but grimaced instead and choked down a mouthful of recovery goop from a pouch.

"Do you have to say that every cycle? How is it you always wake up ahead of me anyways?"

Namuk helped Tali to stand.

"The system just likes my genes better, whips 'em up real fast."

Tali laughed and then groaned at the pain as new muscles contracted.

"Take it easy," Namuk said.

"Each body seems a bit weaker than the last, don't you think? Must be running low on substitute proteins."

Namuk gave a non-committal grunt.

"Where's Pars?" Tali asked, looking around.

"Already recovered. You know Pars, wanted to get to work in the water reclamation unit."

Tali shuddered.

"Space sludge. Glad it's not me."

Namuk's eyes shifted over to a data interface.

"I've got to work in the control room today. Can you go down to the solar sail array? I got an alert that its efficiency has dropped to below 80% and we need all the power we can get."

"Right. Only five cycles left!" Tali glanced over at the incineration pods before following Namuk into the corridor — one still blinked red. "Maybe when we get home, they'll be able to cure this virus so we can keep these bodies."

Tali grinned at Namuk who looked away, not answering.

They separated at a junction, Tali heading down to the solar array and Namuk hurrying up to Command.

Curious, Tali hesitated before making a final turn and glanced back up the hall. Sure enough, Namuk took the left corridor that led to the bridge. But Tali couldn't shake the feeling something wasn't quite right. The other crewmate had looked drawn, almost haggard, and though that could be from putting too much stress too soon on the new body, it seemed deeper than that.

Tali bent over the solar console and began diagnostics. Almost immediately, the system reported back its findings. The result was nothing Tali had been expecting. Their solar array was performing right on schedule based on its lifetime usage statistics. Tali's heart missed a beat as the data built into a virtual model. The usage charts showed the system was nearing its hundredth cycle.

"That can't be right," Tali murmured.

They had left the station only 36 cycles ago and the contamination event on the uncharted moon they were mapping had occurred only 15 cycles ago.

Tali ran the report again. And then a third time. A tingle of dread reverberated through every bone in the new body.

Tali forced a deep breath and raised a comm cuff.

"Pars? Namuk? Do you copy?"

Neither responded.

Tali linked the data to an internal storage port and rushed out of the maintenance hatch. The water reclamation room was closer than Command. Instead of finding Pars hard at work battling space sludge, the room sat empty.

"Pars?" Tali shouted, scanning the empty corridors.

No sign of anyone.

The valve log showed it hadn't been accessed on today's cycle as expected but oddly registered a cleanout yesterday.

Bewildered, Tali hurried up toward the Command deck, keeping an eye out for Pars. But the ship remained silent and empty. To Tali's relief, Namuk sat in the control room, facing away from the corridor, surrounded by the normal array of telemetry readings.

"I can't find Pars anywhere and the valve room log shows we cleaned it out yesterday," Tali panted, coming to a halt just within the door. "But that can't be right, can it? Didn't we reconfigure the Medbay systems all last cycle?"

Drawing closer, Tali hesitated. Namuk's eyes remained closed. A small recycler sat on a table with tubes connecting to bioports in the crooks of each arm. A steady stream of nanobots flowed out of one port, into the recycler and back out the other side.

"What are you doing?" Tali reached out, prodding an arm.

Namuk came awake with a start, reflexively covering the box with a clawed hand.

"Why are you up here?" Namuk slurred.

"Are you using nanos? That's beyond reckless."

"Don't you think I know that?" Namuk's face hardened for a moment before relenting. "I need them to flush the virus."

"But you shouldn't need that, not until tonight's cycle." Tali glanced between Namuk's gaunt face and the nanos as they ebbed and finally finished their job with a soft whirring. "You haven't been switching bodies, have you?"

Namuk began to disassemble the machine, not meeting Tali's eyes.

"There isn't enough supplies. I had to choose. So, you've been getting a body every cycle, and I've been going every other cycle."

"Does Pars know what you're doing?"

"Pars is gone," Namuk whispered, not looking up but instead carefully placing the recycler onto the console between them. "Consciousness and body never reconnected after cycle fifty."

"What? No … Pars was fine just last cycle." Tali took a step back, reeling. "And we've only been traveling for fifteen cycles, not fifty …"

"See for yourself."

Namuk pulled up the ship's scanners. Two bio signatures blinked to life on the overlay of the ship metrics.

"No," Tali whispered.

But there was no doubting the haunted look in Namuk's eyes. None of it made any sense, not the solar array data or valve logs. Now a crew member who just yesterday was helping repair the med bay had died tens of cycles ago.

Tali swallowed hard.

"We're not heading home, are we?"

"No."

Namuk answered in a hoarse voice.

"You've been lying to me all this time, resetting me to the cycle before so I wouldn't catch on? How could you?"

"They were going to kill us, Tali." Namuk whispered.

"What do you mean?"

"Home, our own people … they couldn't risk infecting the rest of the fleet."

"You don't know that." Tali trembled, fighting against the urge to yell.

"I do," Namuk said. "I heard them when they scanned us on cycle thirty."

"But the virus only transfers organically. Once we remotely linked into new bodies, we'd be clean."

"There's a chance the virus mutated to match our structures." Namuk finally met Tali's eyes. "Why else did Pars' consciousness stop making the transition?"

Horror ripped through Tali, quickly replaced by fear.

"Have you tested it?"

Namuk shrugged and sank onto the floor.

Tali leaned over a console, frantically trying to run new stats.

"This ship isn't supplied for long-term body regrowth. Even if you've stopped using your share, we shouldn't have even lasted this long."

"I recalibrated the chambers so they would take less material."

"How long do we have?" Tali asked after a long silence.

Namuk grimaced.

"I'm not sure. I've just been taking it one cycle at a time, hoping something will come along, a ship or a planet, with the resources we need."

Tali sank down to sit next to Namuk.

"Is there even anything out this far?"

"Not sure." Namuk shrugged. "This is uncharted space, way outside exploration parameters."

The overhead lights began to pulse red, signifying another cycle's end and urging them to the incineration chambers to discard their virus-riddled bodies for freshly grown ones.

"You should go," Namuk said.

Tali tried to laugh but a choked sob echoed out instead.

"No. I don't want my memory reset back to yesterday. We're in this together. Plus," Tali shifted, "this latest body isn't all that great. I feel like my bones are rubbing together."

Namuk smiled faintly, too tired to argue and nestled onto Tali's shoulder. Tali welcomed the respite, leaning back against the console behind them, eyelids heavy.

An alert broke the silence.

Tali shook Namuk who slumped, barely breathing. Rising on shaking legs, Tali connected to the nearest interface.

A vessel had entered the ship's scanner range. Though the make of the strange vessel was not logged in the database, it seemed to be a cargo hauler with a large hold full of supplies.

Tali delved deeper, expecting to be rebuffed by a security protocol at any point but the alien vessel was surprisingly unprotected. Better still, it looked to be mostly unarmed, its few projectile weapons impractical against Tali's ship.

Hope began to take hold as the contents of the alien cargo became clearer with each scan. Tali pushed further until a complete manifest formed. One probe reported back that the Medbay on the alien vessel was small but held a large laboratory. Tali hesitated, mulling over the options and looked over at Namuk, stretched unconscious on the floor.

"If you were awake right now," Tali whispered, "you'd try to talk me out of this. But it's my turn to take care of you."

Tali tapped a comm interface and entered the telemetry.

* * *

"Captain, an alert just sounded," Val said over the radio.

"What is it?" Uma asked.

She only half-listened to her first officer, moving a pawn toward the opposing king, as bored as she ever remembered being in twenty years of hauling cargo. The solitude of working with a skeleton crew had its benefits, but five trips in a row were starting to wear on her.

"It's coming from airlock B. I don't understand. It's a docking sequence."

Uma straightened in her seat.

"A malfunction?"

"I'm not sure." Panic began to edge into her first officer's voice. "We never got a proximity alert and I'm not seeing any vessels on our scans."

"Meet me there and bring Basil."

Uma zipped on her boots, preempting the argument she knew that order would bring.

The two crew members were standing in front of the large airlock as she rounded the corner. Basil ignored her as usual. Uma had learned by now not to take his reclusiveness personally.

"Status?" she asked.

"The malfunction doesn't seem to be with the airlock sensors," Val said.

"Are you saying that a ship is actually docked?" Uma asked, eyes narrowing.

"Yes," Val said. "Camera feeds on the outer doors confirm a ship of unknown origin."

Uma stepped up closer.

"So, you're telling me that this ship is not only undetectable, but it's somehow docked without triggering any security protocols?"

Val nodded.

"Impossible." she said.

Uma studied Val, eyeing her first officer and hoping her apparent nervousness wasn't a precursor to mutiny. Before she formulated a question to interrogate her further, however, Basil spoke up.

"The real question," he said. "Isn't how, but what?"

Uma and Val both focused their attention on him. He hadn't spoken more than a handful of words during their voyage thus far.

"Tell her," Basil said, his eyes never leaving the airlock.

Val opened her mouth but quickly closed it again and cleared her throat.

Uma waved.

"Speak freely."

"I saw something when I ran the camera feed." Val paused. "The crew doesn't look human."

A shiver rippled down Uma's spine.

"Show me."

It took all her training and experience to remain calm as she watched the replay.

The screen showed a long corridor, circular in shape with no discernable floor or ceiling.

"I don't see anything," she began.

Uma paused when a red pulsing light began to flicker on the screen, bathing the corridor. As it pulsed, a shadow moved along it, disappearing when the red flashed off and appearing again when it flashed on. The incorporeal figure made it halfway down the hall before the red lights flashed off for a final time. It scurried around the circular corridor.

Uma handed the screen back to Val, cold sweat beading along her neck.

"Have you communicated with them?"

"No, the feed cuts out after that."

Uma walked to the inner door.

"Initiate the comm."

"But we don't know anything about these creatures," Val began, stepping to intercept her. "What if —"

She fell silent when Uma glared at her first officer.

"Basil," she called quietly.

He looked up.

"Yes?"

"What does SEQ have to say about this?"

"Captain?" Basil asked.

Now it was Basil's turn to blanch at the captain's stare.

"Are you or are you not our Code Didact?" she asked.

"Yes, of course. Sorry, I —"

She nodded.

"Well, SEQ," he glanced at Val, "that is Sentient Equality Qualifications, is very specific. The protocols surrounding interactions with sentient lifeforms fall into two main categories, historical and anthropological ..."

He trailed off as Uma began rubbing her temples.

"Basil, I'm going to ask you, just this once. Keep it brief."

He cleared his throat nervously.

"First, we have to qualify these ..." he stumbled at the word *creatures,* "... *beings* as sentient."

"And how do we do that?"

"The criteria are vast but, in this case, I believe we can skip the basic qualifications and look at the final tier."

"Go on ..."

Basil gestured toward the other side of the airlock as if it were obvious.

"They're complex enough to have survived space travel."

The captain nodded, some tightness in her stance relaxing.

"And the final criteria?"

"Compromise."

The captain lifted her eyebrows in question.

"Among other tests," Basil hurried on, "the ability for a lifeform to come to a decision where it neither wins nor loses proves not only critical thinking but the basis for morality, species preservation, and, in all other respects, sentience."

The airlock grew silent as the three ship mates mulled this over.

The captain's eyes darted between her small crew. She had come to a decision.

"I think these newcomers proved their ability to compromise when they chose not to blast open the door and eat our insides, don't you agree?"

Basil began to smile. Then, realizing she wasn't joking, he covered his mouth with a hand.

"They obviously need something from us," Uma continued. "And instead of forcing the issue, they're compromising. So, now that we can confirm that they possess the gift of restraint, Didact, what do we do?"

Basil gripped his hands into fists behind his back to keep them from shaking. His mind yo-yoed between hysteria and torpor. This was more than he'd bargained for when he'd joined the Bellwether. Ten quiet routes running cargo and then he'd be free to choose his own posting. It had seemed more than worth the time, but now, he wasn't so sure.

"SEQ requires the preservation of all sentient life," he recited from the manual.

The captain nodded and, with growing realization, Basil saw she'd had him come to this conclusion aloud, not for her to make an informed judgment, but for the benefit of that stubborn first officer, Val. A trickle of fear ran along his exposed skin as he noticed just how still the young first officer stood, closest to the decompression button. In the short time he'd known her, she'd been quick to anger and uncompromising. But she did follow orders. He lowered his eyes before Val noticed his stare.

"Val," the captain said, "initiate response."

Without hesitation, Val input her access code into the airlock. Static gave way to echoing silence.

"Newcomers." The captain's voice radiated out into the void beyond the airlock. "We are the crew of the Bellwether, and we welcome you to this sector."

Basil fidgeted but Val only had eyes for the captain who waited, letting the silence linger.

When the response came, it didn't come through the speaker to the right of the airlock door. Instead, a crisp, mechanical voice spoke to them from their personal communication links implanted along their left ears.

"Thank you," it said.

They all jumped. Val clutched her ear as if to physically shut the voice out. She shook her head, eyes clenched shut.

"How did it get control of our private biolinks?" Basil whispered.

Uma, eyes wide, made a calming gesture with one hand while motioning from her mouth to her ear with the other, her meaning clear: *It can hear you.*

Basil hesitated, his hand halfway up to his own ear. A sense of purpose settled over him and he stepped forward.

"What should we call you — Newcomer?"

He met the captain's questioning glance with a raised eyebrow, as if to say, *I am the Code Didact after all.*

"I am still compiling your lexicon," the voice said. *"Newcomer* suits for now."

Basil swallowed hard and closed his eyes, trying to concentrate.

"Why have you come to us?"

"I wish to meet face to face."

"I'm afraid we have protocols against that." Uma stepped forward and gestured to Val who was already entering in the locking sequence. The hull's outer airlock hatch began to flash a warning. Their outer airlock door was about to cycle open.

"Captain?" Val asked, stricken, but still punching in codes to the now blank interface.

"They have control of our systems." Uma turned to hear doors creaking open. "Take Basil to the bridge. Secure yourselves and log this into Control. Await their communication. I'll remain here." Uma hoped her face betrayed none of the terror and excitement flowing through her.

Without another question, Val took Basil's arm and half-dragged him out into the corridor. Basil spun, stumbling into a run. The first officer hesitated, conflict pinching her face.

"Go, Val. Do what you can."

Val backed away before turning and running after Basil.

Uma turned and faced the inner airlock door, now partially open. The strange ship's circular corridor blazed red from the other side. She saw no sign of the shadowed being from the feed. Uma's skin prickled.

"Hello?"

Her whisper echoed back to her.

She took a step forward and then another until she stood before the corridor's yawning mouth. At first, she couldn't place why, but something felt off. No change in pressure or temperature occurred with the opening into the other ship. Even the minty smell of the auto disinfectants remained the same as she'd always known.

It seemed like Uma was looking at a hyper-realistic painting. Her fingers reached out toward it only to be met with a barrier. Hairs on the back of her arms stood out at the invisible wall's slight electric charge.

"Are you the captain?"

Uma spun to see the outline of a figure between her and the airlock door leading to the rest of the Bellwether. She took a step back. The being, her height and oddly similar to her in proportion, was more of an outline, a shadow, than a fully-fledged being. It flickered as it spoke directly into the interface on her earlobe.

Uma nodded and, realizing her mouth was hanging open, promptly closed it. When she regained a small measure of her wits, she let herself speak.

"Yes. I am Uma."

"Hello, Uma." The being kept its distance. Whether out of politeness or necessity, Uma was unsure. "I am called Tali."

She tried to regain her former composure and straightened, one hand pressing down the comm button behind her while hoping the others had made it to the bridge and could now hear her through their shared link.

"You've taken control of our ship."

Tali flickered.

"Yes."

"We have protocols we must follow. If you mean us no harm, then please release us."

"There is no threat."

Uma cocked her head.

"What do you really want?" she asked. "Why even speak to us if you're able to do anything you please?"

The being mimicked her action, cocking its slightly oval head.

"Your lab," Tali asked, "what is it for?"

Uma hesitated.

"What do you mean?"

"Why does a cargo ship have a lab?" Tali spoke slower, as if with forced patience.

"Oh."

Uma hesitated, wondering what this information could mean to the survival of her crew and decided on honesty in hopes of reciprocation.

"Well, a lot of our cargo are components that would corrode on the long hauls we pull so we have to keep them isolated and sometimes mix or manufacture the final product on the last leg."

Tali seemed to ponder this, flickering for a moment, its shape dissipating to a vague haze where it remained, unmoving.

Uma stepped forward, steeling herself for whatever that move might convey to the being, but she found she couldn't contain her curiosity.

"Excuse me for asking, but are you okay?"

The being burned bright for a moment and Uma hurried on.

"It's just, you keep flickering. Or is that your natural state?"

"Are you studying me?" Tali asked, more metal in the otherwise toneless voice.

The captain felt a shiver of cold apprehension but the allure of the unknown and its potential promise of death returned to her the resolve she normally carried with her even in the times before she'd become captain.

"Of course," she confessed. "It's hard not to. We've never met anything other than *us*. Isn't that why you're here — to make contact, to learn about humans?"

"No."

"But you said yours was a mission of exploration." Uma crossed her arms. "How do you know so much about us?"

"Necessity."

Tali flickered opaque again and almost went dark.

Uma closed the gap between them until she could almost feel the energy seeping out from the humanoid shape. Deep in the recesses of her intuition, a warning bell sounded. This time, she didn't fear for her own safety, but for Tali's.

"You need help?" she asked.

Tali's mechanical voice seemed to sigh in resignation.

"Components."

"What?" Uma asked, thinking she'd misheard.

"We need components from your lab."

Uma clenched her jaw, processing the potential deception.

Tali seemed to read her apprehension.

"You don't believe me."

"It's just, well, you don't look like, you know, would have any use for physical …" Uma hesitated, feeling for one dizzying moment, as though she didn't want to offend this alien, "… stuff," she finished lamely, gesturing to Tali's buzzing outline. "Plus, you're far more advanced than us."

"Complex structures are just as susceptible as simple ones …" Tali said, letting her words trail off.

Uma paced the few steps afforded to her in the small airlock, contemplating her next move. She wished she had Basil here beside her. This was his whole point for being forced onto them after all. No captain liked having a useless crew member, but company policy dictated the presence of a Code specialist on long hauls through dead space to assuage any moral liability. She glanced at the being who seemed to wait patiently.

"Basil," Uma called out, directing her voice to the comm speaker by the airlock seal.

"Yes, we're here."

Basil's voice sounded thin and reedy even by his standards.

"Did you catch any of that?"

"Yes. The life form needs help?"

"I believe so."

"Tali," Basil shouted. "How much of our components do you need?"

"I have shared our requisites with your vessel."

Data readouts popped up on every display in the ship. Uma blinked at the nearest one. They were simple protein structures.

"And you need us to mix these for you?"

"Yes."

"Captain," Val butted in over the commlink. "May I speak with you?" She hesitated. "In private?"

Uma glanced over at Tali.

"I don't think there is such a thing as privacy anymore, Val. Whatever you have to say, be quick about it."

"These would use up a good deal of our supplies," Val's voice sounded peevish.

"Your cargo," Tali corrected.

"Yes, exactly, our livelihood. We'd have to accrue a loss even after all the effort —"

"What?" Basil cut in. "How can you even think about money when a new life form is asking for help?"

"It's not a *new* lifeform. It's just *new* to us and perfectly capable of —"

"Enough." Uma said, rubbing the bridge of her nose in resigned frustration.

She'd spent six weeks with her crew of two and they were as different from one another as could be. But one thing they all had in common was their stubborn sense of duty. Uma had come to a decision whether or not Val liked it or agreed with it.

"Alright," she continued, "these demands seem reasonable. We're more than happy to help. Val, direct the lab mechs to begin work."

"How soon will the materials be ready?" Tali asked, shifting slightly.

"Ten minutes, maybe less," Val interjected.

Uma glanced at the still flickering life form.

"Do you need to sit or rest … or something?"

"This body is a projection," Tali answered simply. "I curated it to match you."

"So, you don't really look like this?" Uma asked.

There was a beat of silence.

"Did you really think that in all the cosmos, sentient life not only evolved twice within the same time and within close enough proximity as to chance upon each other in the short duration where we each develop interplanetary travel, and we just so happen to look alike?"

"Er – No?" Uma smirked. "So what do you and your fellow beings look like, may I ask?"

Tali flickered for a moment before shifting into a large grub.

Uma tilted her head, thinking Tali looked like a tardigrade. She bit back nervous laughter.

Tali shifted back.

"We appreciate your assistance."

"Why do you need our help, if you're so advanced?" Val said over the speaker.

Uma pinched the bridge of her nose.

"Val," she began.

"Our bodies should not leave our vessels," Tali said.

Whatever answer she was expecting, it had not been that.

"You can only live on your ships?" Uma asked.

Tali paused.

"This is probably outside your scope."

"Try us," Basil said with a bit too much enthusiasm from the intercom.

"We transmit our consciousness supra corporeally."

"Like a computer?" Basil asked.

Tali flickered darker.

"No."

"Sorry if that was wrong," Uma interjected. "You're right, we have no context here. But we are willing to learn."

"I'll try to explain" Tali said. "Our biological makeup is only a portion of our existence. Unlike your form, ours don't last long enough to make use of life. Long ago, too long to count, we developed a way to store our consciousness. Unlike what you call a computer, it does not become electronic signals that rely on charged particles. It is more chemical. As water turns to ice or vapor under rigorous conditions, our consciousness can coalesce or dissipate."

"But you still use bodies?"

Uma felt perplexed by the process Tali described.

"Yes."

"Couldn't you just ... exist?" she asked.

"No. That breeds madness. But we weren't always like this." Tali grew more opaque as if to make her point. Uma could almost make out the ghosts of eyes in the otherwise nondescript face. "Our thoughts need grounding in biological connections. Plus, corporeal existence is more fun."

Uma found herself smiling, some of the tension easing. Tali flickered for a moment and then went out.

"Tali?" Uma called.

"I'm fading." The voice was only a whisper now. "Help ..."

"Val, how much longer?"

"First batch ready."

Uma nodded.

"Meet me at the airlock as soon as you get it."

"Captain —" Val began.

"Go," Uma cut her off. "That's an order."

Basil ran around the corner, sliding into the airlock.

"What are you doing?" she asked.

"You'll suit up faster if you have help." Basil's voice was now calm, holding none of his usual nervous energy.

They began to fumble with the tactical suits set within an alcove of the corridor. She hesitated only a moment before breaking the emergency seals on one tailored to her specifications. An alarm blared on the station's biolinks. Uma shut it off with her code sequence.

Without being asked, Basil began to tap in the sequences to prep the suit.

Uma glanced over at him, bewildered.

"How do you know the atmosphere composition of the alien ship?"

"What do you think Val was doing while you were busy chatting?"

He allowed a momentary smirk before his brow furrowed again in concentration.

"Val was able to probe their ship?" Uma asked, pride and fear mingling. "That could've backfired. What if they'd been hostile?"

Basil shrugged.

"There's no reasoning with Val."

Uma slid into the suit, allowing Basil to clamp on the gloves and boots.

"Val, where are we on the materials?" she called.

"Heading your way," came the grudging response.

"Make it fast."

Uma turned to Basil who held her helmet.

They both turned back to the jammed open airlock revealing the interior of the oval corridor within Tali's ship. Uma remembered the feel of the rough surface of the illusion when she tried to push a hand through it earlier.

He hesitated.

"How are you going to get in?"

"Any ideas?" she asked.

"I have one." Val jogged up to them, carrying a small crate.

"What is this?" Uma gave her a searching look.

Val shrugged.

"It's all the bots could synthesize this fast. But it's better than nothing."

Uma relented and waved to the open airlock.

"That's just an illusion."

"Right," Val said. "I noticed when I probed the ship. But I think there's something behind it. Look at this."

She handed the box of supplies to Uma and walked over to the open hatch. Val took out the utility weapon she carried with her and used the mag light on the end to shine into the illusion. Wherever the light touched, the illusion faded to reveal a small, solid-looking door. It shone black.

They drew in a collective breath as the door began to shift. An alarm sounded. The airlock door began to reactivate.

"Hurry!" Uma shouted. "It's closing."

Basil attached her helmet before Val dragged him out just as the airlock doors slid shut.

Without Val's light, all Uma saw was the illusion glowing.

"Is everyone okay?" she asked, her comms crackling.

"Yes, we're here on the other side." Val said.

"Good luck," Basil added.

Uma raised her free hand to her helmet, activating its thermal lights.

"I'll radio when I'm back."

The illusion disappeared to reveal a cramped doorway, now open. She worried she wouldn't fit through in her bulky suit. With a deep breath, she walked toward it and poked her head inside.

The corridor resembled the one displayed on the illusion; a circular tunnel blinking red. Uma tried to even out her breaths as she moved through the small space. Blinking floor lights guided her until she reached what looked to be a small command room. A being lay on the floor, unmoving. It resembled a grub with two claws curling out from each of its six legs. Its exoskeleton was almost translucent with organ-like structures pulsing within. Uma moved carefully. In a long, cocoon-like chair in the middle of the room rested another one. This one had its eyes opened and turned toward her, a small box with tubes whirred nearby.

"When I awoke this cycle, I never thought I'd encounter aliens," Tali whispered through Uma's comm connection, its circular mouth unmoving. "Or that I'd allow one into our sanctum."

"I'm here to help," Uma said. She held the box of supplies out before her. "What do I need to do?"

"There."

Tali nodded over to a chute.

A trickle of nervous sweat beaded on Uma's forehead. She crab-walked over to the far wall and glanced back at Tali before she emptied the canister. A gong sounded in the small room.

"Did I do the right thing?" Uma asked, heart racing.

"Yes, the recycler will take it from here," Tali said. "We just need one more thing from you."

Uma turned.

"What?"

"Take our bodies to the pods"

"Where are they?"

Uma began to shake.

"Follow the lights," Tali said, her voicing trailing to a whisper.

The corridor outside the command room, which flickered red before, now pulsed in a quick blue glow leading out and away.

Uma crawled over to the first being that lay unconscious. "Sorry," she said, scooping up the small body and carrying it over to Tali who attempted to move closer but instead flopped onto the floor.

"Oof." Uma grimaced. "Here, let me help."

She wedged Tali under her other arm and began to crabwalk as quickly as her stiff suit allowed out into the corridor. She tried not to bang either of the creatures on the walls.

The blue lights led her into a small room with a series of pods. Two stood open. One was closed and blinking red. On instinct, Uma placed a body in each open pod, hoping Tali was still lucid enough to tell her otherwise.

"Thank you," Tali said.

Uma reached down to touch what she thought of as Tali's hand.

"This is the only way to destroy the virus."

Uma pulled back in horror. A small, ring-like object slid off the wrist of one of Tali's arms and the pod covers shut. Uma backed up, her heart beating a frantic rhythm of panic and hope. An alarm blared and the pods grew bright red with heat. Giving into her panic, she crawled as quickly as she could back out of the passageway and shut the ship's outer door behind her. The airlock began to cycle through its decontamination and re-pressurizing protocols.

"Val, status?" Uma choked out between pants, taking off her gloves.

"Captain! You're back!" Basil called. "What was —"

"Status optimal," Val cut in. "We're ready to receive you once the doors cycle."

"Negative," Uma said. "I'm not sure what just happened. I may have destroyed Tali and her crew mate. But before that happened," she rushed on as she could practically hear Basil's question coming, "I think Tali said something about a virus."

"A virus?" Val repeated.

"Yes. To be safe, I'm enacting quarantine protocols."

Uma tapped out the commands on her wrist interface.

"Was this in the training vids? I don't remember anything about quarantine …" Uma heard Basil whisper to Val.

"The doors won't open until the systems verify that there are no pathogens." Val said. "Captain, there's something else. We've received word back from the nearest outpost. They're sending a representative ship."

Uma removed her helmet.

"How long?"

"An hour," Val said.

Uma remained quiet, her forehead clammy beneath her fingers.

"Captain, you've done nothing wrong," Basil broke in. "The Code states —"

"They won't care about the Code," Val said, cutting him off.

"But they must …"

Basil trailed off without finishing his thought.

"Not if there's risk of a pathogen," Uma confirmed, biting back a groan. "They'll read the quarantine status of our ship along with my logs."

"And incinerate us," Val concluded.

"No," Basil said. "There must be something we can do."

Uma shook her head, glad her crew couldn't see her in this part of the airlock. She looked down at the small ring-like object she'd pulled from Tali's body.

"We wait."

A faint voice pricked her senses. It came not from within the biolink which Tali had spoken through just moments ago, but out of the alien ring she gripped in her fist. Shocked, Uma almost dropped the ring. The tighter she clutched it, the clearer the voices were until, with her knuckles white, two voices, sharp and clear, reverberated through her.

* * *

On the other side of the airlock door, Tali and Namuk awoke within their grow chambers. Tali first pulled free, panting with the pain of new muscles, and slid on newly synthesized comm cuffs. The other body began to wriggle with life.

"Namuk?" Tali called.

Namuk groaned, gripping another set of cuffs.

"What happened ... how?"

"You were right," Tali said, handing over a recovery pouch and downing the goop from another. "We encountered an alien vessel that had the right compilation of proteins."

"A ship?" Namuk asked, hopeful. "And you were able to take what we need?"

"Yes. They helped us."

Namuk choked on the goo and spluttered.

"You met them?"

Tali bristled.

"I had no choice; my body was already failing."

"But they could have infiltrated our systems! Our maps would lead them back to the station."

"They're not like us," Tali said.

Namuk sat back.

"There's something I want to show you." Tali walked over to the nearest interface and linked in.

Namuk followed. It only took moments, but once all the data arrayed itself, a look of dawning comprehension began to form. Namuk, awestruck, nodded. "Lead on."

* * *

Within the airlock, Uma sat with her head in her hands while her thoughts circled the problem she had forced upon her crew. There had been no further communication from the incoming command fleet. Val had refused all direct orders to take an escape pod and distance themselves from the quarantined Bellwether while Basil had sequestered himself in his small berth, composing Insight Entries, the loudest call to arms his vocation allowed.

"Uma?" Tali asked.

Uma brought her head up with a jolt. The opaque outline of two beings stood in front of her. She stood and fell back against the wall.

"Tali?" she asked. "Did it work?"

"You didn't think we'd survive?" Tali asked. "This is Namuk."

One flickered slightly.

Uma nodded.

"Nice to meet you. But we're in a bit of a bind actually. You may want to disconnect from our airlock."

"We know all about your quarantine. It is unnecessary."

There was no discernable difference in tone between the two voices, but Uma thought this newcomer, Namuk, spoke in a clipped way, as if used to giving orders.

"But the virus —" Uma began.

"It has mutated past the point where cross-contamination is possible," Tali said.

"So, I'm not infected?" Uma's heart beat fast.

"It seems it's uniquely adapted to our structures." Namuk said, glowing brighter.

"I see."

Uma glanced at the speaker set into the airlock wall.

"We've disabled your communications equipment for now," Namuk said, guessing at Uma's thoughts. "Your crew is fine. But we do have one thing more to ask of you."

"This may help us all," Tali said.

Uma swallowed, trying to compose herself, and nodded.

"Okay. What is it?"

"We need your vessel." Namuk stated.

"After you've launched the escape pod, of course," Tali added.

Uma looked between them, unease growing into horror.

"I'm sorry, what?"

"As Basil said, survival of sentient life must take precedent."

Uma narrowed her eyes.

"You seem very much alive to me."

"We believe there's a way to get our third crew member back," Tali admitted.

"You lost someone to the virus?" Uma asked.

"Before we met, yes." Namuk said.

"And how can my ship help?"

"Your inferior —" Namuk began.

"The technology aboard this vessel is far different from what the virus is used to encountering," Tali said, interrupting. "The Bellwether will be a clean start for our newly regenerated bio-forms."

Uma got a sinking feeling that she didn't have a choice in this. The newcomers had full control of her ship and could have gotten what they needed through force.

"It seems like it's already yours," she said, tamping down a hysterical laugh. "But you won't have it for much longer. My people are coming soon and they're likely to incinerate anything with a quarantine alert."

"Oh, that," Tali said. "We've already sent a communication that the ship's computer systems malfunctioned and that you are currently abandoning the vessel."

Uma's mouth went dry.

"And you think they're going to believe that?"

"We were very convincing," Namuk replied.

"Their sensors will show them everything they need to see," Tali added.

"And nothing of us," Namuk finished.

"Nothing?" Uma was shocked. "But all the communications we sent them?"

"Explained away. Re-coded. Video proof created," Tali said.

"It was quite easy, really," Namuk added.

"But what if my people wanted to meet yours?"

"Perhaps one day." Namuk said, flickering.

"Why not now?" Anger seeped into Uma's voice. "Why not just meet our people? Instead, you leave me trapped, forced to explain something erased from our logs. I'll lose my livelihood, my reputation. With even a small piece of your technology, I could revolutionize everything."

"You were our first contact too," Tali said. "We can't be seen in this weakened state by any more of your kind."

Uma smiled sarcastically.

"The danger of weak things?"

Tali flickered as if laughing.

"Ah, and it looks like your crew is ready to go," Namuk said.

The outer airlock door opened, and Val and Basil stood just without, wearing full suits. Tali and Namuk disappeared.

"Captain?" Val asked. "Are you okay? We received your communication, and the command ship is awaiting the arrival of our evacuation pod."

Uma blinked rapidly in disbelief.

"My communication?"

"Yes." Basil stepped forward, picking up her discarded helmet and gloves and helping her to put them on. "I was able to confirm that your bioscan came back clean, no sign of contagion. But the quarantine protocol seems to have disabled our life support as you said just now."

Uma glanced around but Tali and Namuk were gone. Their plan was working, it would seem.

Val looked at her wrist interface.

"Escape pod ready."

The crew rushed to the escape pod's open hatch.

Just as the doors began to shut, Uma thought she saw a flicker of a figure wave to her from the corridor. She raised her hand halfway up.

"What is it, captain?" Basil asked, looking past her.

"Nothing," she said and turned to him. "What did your reports say about the newcomers, the new life forms?"

Basil sighed.

"It seems that the ship's recordings show nothing during the time Tali visited us. And what's more, the logs show a gas leak that would have definitely caused hallucinations."

"*Group* hallucinations?" Uma asked, feeling incredulous.

Basil shrugged.

"Suggestibility is a big factor the auditors could point to. Tali did the job well." He sighed. "I just wish it had all been worth it."

"What do you mean?" Uma asked.

"Well, like you said to us when you were trapped in the airlock. We were too late. The virus got them anyway."

Uma leaned back as Val piloted the small craft away. Through the window, she watched the Bellwether recede while her fingers tightened on Tali's ring. The faint voices grew stronger as she gripped it harder.

"I bet we could learn a lot from them, and I think we could still teach them a thing or two, even if they did think us unworthy," Uma said.

Val laughed from her pilot's seat.

"I would have liked to prove them wrong."

"Me too," Uma said.

She tapped a spot on her interface and began to record everything she heard within Tali's ring.

Sarah Connell is the author of the cozy science fiction trilogy, Project Awakening, and her stories have appeared in magazines and anthologies across the world. A collector of hobbies, her favorite things outside of books include painting, hiking, and growing obscure vegetables in her garden. She lives in the Carolinas with her person and their cat, Lyra. You can see more about her stories at sarah-connell.com.

VI

Fear the Human

By: Mike Morgan

Fear the Human

Fear the human, for its kindness is death.

Fear the human, my cousins, for its weapons are good intentions.

Fear the human, my cherished ones, for it sees only what it expects.

Above all else, I beg of you, fear the human because it thinks it knows what's right.

* * *

"Keep firing!"

Susie glanced over at Devron, irritated by his obvious statement. Her colleague followed his own orders, raking the pack of snarling, five-legged predators with another burst from his gun. Susie aimed to the right, targeting a group that had broken off from the main cluster, and fired several more rounds.

There had to be nearly a hundred slavering creatures. They'd brought down twenty, maybe twenty-five. Too hard to get an accurate count in the confusion. Plenty were left, that was plain enough, and they were too damn close.

Susie shot one creature as it pounced, her bullets catching it in what she assumed was the creature's face. It had a mouth filled with teeth on the end of its neck, and no other features. She must have struck a vital organ because the creature collapsed to the stony ground, a few scant inches from her.

"We can't hold this position," she shouted.

One of the meat eaters would get through eventually. Like it or not, they were going to have to fall back.

In her peripheral vision, she saw the Artists standing where she'd found them only minutes earlier, hunched on their five limbs, unmoving. Like the carnivores, they followed a pentapedal body plan. Unlike the predators, they were peaceful.

What was wrong with the aliens they'd befriended? Didn't they understand the danger they were in? Susie and Devron couldn't protect them much longer.

Bewildered by their lack of response, she screamed at the Artist clan. "Run! For God's sake, save yourselves!"

* * *

Hear me, hear the sorrows of Crooked Limb.

Hear the rumbling of my words, sent from the echoing drum of my chest to the sensitive spines upon your backs.

I am the Sayer of the Clan of the Fractured Plains. I am Crooked Limb whose rear leg grew as twisted and curved as the spiral of a plant stem.

I am Crooked Limb, who was entrusted with the future of a clan and who failed in that solemn duty.

How right, how just, to cede to me the burden of Sayer. My blood is weak, but my mind is sharp, my memory clearest of all.

How wise to entrust the clan into my care; how fitting the feeblest of body should be the strongest of purpose, the one to preserve the undying flame of All-That-We-Know.

How unexpected the failure; how unspeakable the loss.

Hear me, hear the sorrows of Crooked Limb.

Hear my words of caution, Sayers of distant clans.

Hear my history and mark my failure.

Hear most of all this: fear the human.

For when you encounter it, it seems not the destruction of all that has ever been and all that shall ever be. It hides what it is, even from itself.

* * *

"I don't think they're dangerous."

Susan Hamilton, Susie to her friends, gazed at the herd of pentagon-shaped creatures. She estimated at least three hundred in the herd. Each one appeared to be the size of a cow. At least, the size she imagined a cow would be. She'd never seen one in person. They were rare enough on Earth, and it wasn't like she got back there more than once a decade.

"Good," Devron said over the comm-link. "Because I'm at least fourteen minutes from you. So, don't get in any trouble."

The planetary specialist talked like he was in charge. He so wasn't. Susie held the same rank as Devron Khan, which made them equals on the two-person survey mission.

She edged closer to the herd, recording the sight for later analysis. A stampede seemed unlikely. The creatures were oblivious to her presence, concerned more with grazing on the spiral-shaped vegetation jutting out from between the red rocks.

The animals possessed torsos with five distinct sides, she noted. A leg protruded from the tip of each point. The neck extended from the center of the side that Susie assumed was the front; although, that wasn't necessarily the case as the herbivores seemed to move in any direction with equal ease. Often, they would pause and lift two not-quite-opposite limbs from the rocky terrain in a languid stretch. With five legs, they were able to flex this way without losing their balance. Susie wondered if the ground was hard on their feet.

Samples she'd taken of plant life in the area showed evidence of vegetation rich in protein: an alien quinoa. On Kepler-452b, it seemed, plant eaters enjoyed a high-energy diet with minimal effort. The gravity was 1.2 standard. The air contained a breathable mixture of gases, with temperatures cooler than Earth had enjoyed in many centuries. In every way, this world was a paradise. It even smelled nice. Kepler-452b stood out as the most habitable planet she'd ever surveyed. Sheer travel distance offered the only fly in the ointment. Kepler-452b orbited its parent star more than a thousand light years from humanity's homeworld. Even with the latest gravity drives, that was an eye watering commute.

"Oh, my God," Devron said.

"What?"

"The drones were right."

Susie lowered the omnikit she'd been using to record the herd's gentle munching and started paying attention to what Devron was saying. He'd taken a flyer to one of the deep crevices that scored the threadbare plains, following up on readings taken by autonomous aerial survey units. That's how the Exoplanet Survey and Evaluation Corps — ESEC to its donors — analyzed alien worlds. AI-driven drones did the bulk of the grunt work and small teams of human specialists followed up on anything the machines couldn't understand. In this instance, a drone scanning the crevice had reported markings on the rocks. None of the markings could be accounted for through geological processes.

"Right in what way?" she asked. "The marks there aren't natural?"

"They look like cave paintings to me."

Her mind raced. Devron had to be wrong. Intelligent life was incredibly rare in the galaxy. A treasure to be preserved at all costs when it was found. But no, he had to jump to conclusions. She made a point of not leaping ahead of the evidence in the field. Being wrong was too easy.

"What are the paintings of?"

Dammit, why didn't the idiot turn on his own omnikit and show her?

"I'm looking at hundreds of pictures of those five-legged cows of yours," he said over the comm-link.

Susie glanced back at the herd. The creatures kept chewing.

* * *

Hear me, cousins, you Sayers of distant clans: we did not know.

We did not know.

In our ignorance, we dwelt with the two-legs in fellowship upon the Fractured Plains. Our hearts were tranquil, for we did not yet understand.

How strange they seemed.

How unsteady on two limbs.

One was smaller than the other, as if still half grown. Atop the bulbous tops of their bodies, both sported tufts of a featherless down like the protective coats of ripening pods. The down of the larger one was shorter than the down of the smaller stranger.

They roamed ever in the company of glittering flying sprites, each no larger than the biting pests that come in the warm season. The two-legs seemed to be masters of these sprites; the hovering, thrumming things came and went at their call, for what purpose we could not tell.

Long the two-legs stood near the Great Tally. Did they count the numbers of the cycles? I cannot say. Even now, I cannot say.

We sent echoing calls again and again from our reverberating chest cavities, yet they heard us not. They had no spines upon their flesh with which to hear, and we knew sorrow at the deafness that must be their lot. How terrible to not feel sound in a world so filled with it.

If simple communication was not possible, we decreed, we would learn more of our new friends through watchfulness and calm contemplation of their actions.

All the while, as we observed these visitors, we pondered a deeper question: Where did these two-legs come from? The universe was the World and the Sleeping. There were no other parts to it than those.

If they came not from the World, were they dreams from the Sleep? Had they seeped into our waking years and clad themselves in substance? If that were so, what would a dream want of us?

Our time on the Fractured Plains neared an end. The bellies of my clanspeople were almost full, the pods within our undersides so large they had no more space to grow. Soon, we would walk to the hills and the high pass between the mountains.

Soon, we would leave. And when I, Crooked Limb, returned, I would go to the place where the land broke apart. There I would crush the red rocks and mix the dust with water and draw the symbol that was me on the Great Tally, so those who remained would not forget the time we transitioned from one cycle to the next.

What the two-legs would do, I could not say. Perhaps they, too, carried pods. Perhaps they would come with us and wait for the sharp-toothed change.

How natural that would have been, Sayers of other clans, how right. That was not to be.

* * *

"Don't laugh," Susie said. "I think they're talking."

She felt the campfire's warmth envelop her face, a welcome sensation

114

in the cool morning air. Susie and Devron were finishing breakfast at their small, minimum-impact encampment.

Knowing full well who 'they' were, Devron seized on the chance to let her know how wrong she was.

"There are a million ways organisms communicate," he snapped. "Every planet we've found with life, we've discovered a new way information gets transferred. Talking? Why would they talk when they're not from Earth? Speaking is a terrestrial thing to do. And we'd know if they could talk after studying them for three weeks."

He upended his mug, tipping the dregs into a waste can. Every scrap of refuse they generated had to be bagged and shipped off-planet. No contaminating the biosphere, not during the survey. No despoiling an alien ecology until the right bribes were paid and the land was sold. Whatever the future held for this world, the surveyors would not be the ones who tainted it.

Susie sucked in a breath and blew it back out with a hint of irritation.

"If I'm right, they've been speaking to us the whole time and we've not realized."

Her fellow specialist frowned, looking like he planned to fill the air with his endless opinions. That's what Devron did. When he thought people were about to say something that contradicted him or would paint him in anything less than a stellar light, he'd start talking over the top of them and keep on going, spewing words until his listeners gave up from sheer exhaustion. Devron had a gift, there was no denying it. He could say nothing at all for hours on end.

"That rumbling noise they make—it's possible there's an ultrasonic component to it." Susie continued with some haste, keeping him from jumping in and taking over the conversation. "We can't hear frequencies above twenty kilohertz and the omnikits don't scan for them in the default checklist. I've been wondering how these creatures can sense the environment when they don't have eyes and

I'm becoming more and more convinced it's through echolocation. If they're navigating with ultrasound, they could be communicating with it too, at least partially. I think we've not detected language because we've only been picking up a fraction of what they're saying."

Susie lifted her omni and changed its settings.

"It's easy enough to adjust for," she added. "If I'm right, we should be able to get enough samples of their vocalizations to build a prototype translation algorithm in just a few hours."

She understood Devron's doubts. Using sound of any type to communicate was a peculiarly Earth-type thing to do. Yet the five-legged creatures had to be exchanging thoughts and ideas somehow. The paintings offered solid evidence they were intelligent beings.

Devron arched an eyebrow as he grabbed a folding shovel and a baggie. Judging from the equipment he'd gathered, she figured he was heading behind the tangle of vegetation to dig what they delicately called a 'poo hole.' What couldn't be bagged up would be buried. Gross, but a fact of life in the field.

"Fine," he ceded without enthusiasm. "Assuming they share our enthusiasm for chit-chatting, what are you going to say to them?"

First contact situations hardly ever happened. Protocols in the field manual, though, covered these scenarios.

"I thought I'd start with the basics," Susie said. "You know, ask what they're called. Tell them we're human. Make sure they get that we mean them no harm."

"Sounds terrific." He ambled away. "Can't wait to learn all about them. I'm sure they have some amazing insights into the best tasting plant life in the area."

Devron acting like her idea was terrible wasn't surprising. After all, he hadn't been the one to think of it.

* * *

Long did I converse with the smaller of the two-legs. As slow as limbs growing strong and supple after sleep fades, the meaning of their calls became clear.

Human, I learnt they were named.

They placed importance on naming things and others. For the human, an object or person did not, could not, exist without a name.

"Tell us who you are," pleaded the small human, the one who wanted to feel the shape of our thoughts.

"We are us," I said.

"But what are you called?" it replied.

"We are the clan that dwells here."

Was this not obvious?

"Your group must have a name," it insisted.

My hunger was not as great as my fellow clanspeople. No pod grew within my underside; the nub was shriveled and dry, undone by the same deficiency that had twisted my leg. So, I paused in my grazing and spoke with the human, though its words were without reason.

"When I meet with the Sayers of other places, I describe where we dwell. This is the plain of many fractures. That is where we are now, who we are now."

"Where you are now? Are you going somewhere else?"

I told the human of our journey, the long trek on which we were about to set forth.

"Can we come with you?" it asked.

Forgive me, Sayers, for I said yes.

* * *

Devron was in a foul mood, Susie could tell. He wasn't enjoying accompanying the natives on their migration.

The walk across the edge of the plain had been gentle enough. Susie and Devron packed up their camp and loaded it on the flyer. They sent the craft ahead, removing the need to lug along any supplies as they trudged over stony, plant-studded terrain. But the ground didn't stay flat. After a few hours, the land turned hillier and distant mountains broke through the mist. Devron's lips tightened at the sight.

"Maybe I should get on the flyer and meet you up ahead," he suggested.

"But we're learning so much about them, the Artists."

That was her name for the natives. They didn't have a clear title for their society, so Susie invented one of her own, inspired by the paintings Devron had discovered. She gestured at the wide group of aliens.

"You don't want to miss anything."

"Don't I?" he muttered.

Susie flashed a frown, and Devron raised a hand upon seeing her irritation.

"Fine. What have you learned, exactly?"

"Well, I'm not sure what every single word it says means, but I'm pretty certain I'm getting enough to follow the general sense of what it's telling me."

"Right."

His reply stung.

"For one thing, I've learned the mountain pass we're heading toward only thaws out enough in this warm season to be traversable," Susie said, trying to shake off his condescending attitude. "That's why the clan waited until now."

"They're moving to greener pastures?"

"I don't think that's it."

"It's gotta be something important to be worth all this trouble, something like a fresh food source."

Devron made it clear he was gearing up for one of his talk-over-everything-until-he-won sessions. The man never listened.

"It's not that," Susie said, cutting him off before he could launch into a rant. "There's something inside them. Something growing. That's why they're going to the mountains."

She gestured at the one with the malformed back leg.

"That's what it said, anyway."

Devron frowned so deeply Susie imagined she could hear his brain clanking.

"Growing inside them. Babies? Eggs?"

"More like 'seed'. That's what the omni suggested the closest equivalent was. Although, it gave only a fifty-three percent level of confidence to the translation."

"They're reproducing, though."

"I think so."

Devron nodded.

"Basic biological drive. That'd explain the lengths they're going to."

He said it like he was proving a point to her.

"The twisted-leg one said they each carry one seed," Susie explained. "The only one they can ever grow. Sometimes, if they're lucky, they grow two at once. That's how their population increases, by some of them getting double seeds. They get one shot at growing their seeds. That's it. And they've got to carry them to the mountains. The whole group goes, and ... I guess they do what comes naturally. All except the one who talks the most to us, the one with the curled-up leg. It doesn't have a seed. It's sick or something."

"That's a risky reproductive strategy. No wonder the planet's not overrun with them."

Devron's omni pinged with a data packet receipt.

"What's that?"

He shrugged.

"I sent the drones ahead to scout."

"They find anything?"

"Snow melt. Caves. Nothing much."

Susie nodded.

"Good. Sounds safe. Guess that's why the clan goes up there to give birth. All the wildlife must be down here on the plains."

Devron patted the sidearm holstered on his thigh.

"If there is anything up there, we'll have no trouble handling it."

"You know we're only permitted to shoot in the direst circumstances."

"Uh-huh. Leave no sign we were here. I am aware. Didn't come all this way to get eaten, though. We're allowed to defend ourselves. That's all I'm saying."

Susie brushed her fingertips over the grip of her own pistol. Devron was right for once; she doubted anything on this planet could stand up to the firepower they carried.

* * *

I near the end of my tale, cousins. I near the moment of doom.

I take full responsibility. I knew the human did not comprehend.

This is how I knew: At the first dusk of our mountain pilgrimage, the human stopped. They could not continue moving. My clanspeople and I were seized with the urge to move without surcease, but these human were physically weaker than us. I thought they merely required a brief respite. I was wrong.

The small human, the one with long tufts upon its upper extremity, told me they must construct their temporary nests and sleep until dawn.

Yes, my cousins, you heard me clearly. *Sleep.*

I should have killed them there and then, once I knew their sleep was not as ours, that they regarded sacred slumber as a trivial matter, quickly done with.

To my shame, I did not. I thought to leave them at peace in the endless maze of their strangeness. Although they were bizarre aberrations of the natural order, I did not think they could harm us.

I did not fear the human. I should have.

* * *

Susie found Devron setting up camp.

"Okay. Weirdest conversation ever."

He paused in pitching his tent.

"What?"

"The one with the crooked leg — I swear I offended him."

"How?"

"All I said was we needed to rest for the night."

Devron clicked a pole together.

"They're not stopping in the dark?"

"No. The cold season has passed so they don't need to huddle together for warmth, and they don't see using visible light so there's no issue with moving at night. They're pressing on. A short pause every few hours and some quick munching on the local plants is enough for them to keep their strength up."

"Well, they'll just have to deal with the fact that we do need to stop. We'll catch them up in the morning. I can call the flyer for a pickup if we get too far behind."

"I told it that."

"Then what's the problem?"

"I don't know. I said we needed to sleep, like we do every night. It seemed surprised. So, I asked it if it ever went to sleep."

Devron snapped more of his tent frame together.

"Does it? I've never seen one of them asleep. Mind you, not sure I'd know if they were."

"That was the weird part. The translator missed a lot of what it said, but I think they do have that concept, yeah."

"Then why was it upset?"

Susie shrugged, feeling at a loss.

"I don't understand. I thought we were getting on really well. I don't understand at all."

* * *

The human caught up with us as we reached the mountain pass. I had begun my ascent of the ridge, climbing away from the rest of my clanspeople. They were hunkered down, in preparation for what was to come.

My clanspeople chose a good location. Several caves were nearby. The consumers of meat would soon emerge from the torpor brought on by extreme cold. They would be groggy and, most of all, starving.

My thoughts were maudlin as I scaled the ridge to observe what must happen. It was easy to imagine the feelings and sensations my clanspeople would be experiencing. Unbearable constriction around their pods, chests that felt close to tearing open, dull throbbing of nerve connections between pod and forebrain dying in preparation, gradual dimming of thought as those connections atrophied and consciousness retreated to its fortress. Feelings I had shared myself, through many cycles. But no more, no more. With no pod of my own, I was the Sayer for the cycle. No pod condemned me to my end, once this body wore out.

Then, from near the uppermost part of the ridge, I sensed the human enter the mountain pass.

How astonished I was. The human had awoken from their sleep already, just as they said they would.

How was this possible?

To sleep and wake and be full-grown with the warming of each new day?

Our kind, perforce, had to gorge ourselves for many seasons near the end of each cycle to store enough energy for the transition that came with sleep. These humans accomplished the same miracle in mere fractions of a day. They were terrifying.

A sound carried to my back spines. The grumbling snuffle of a cave creature.

Emerging from its den, eager to eat.

Relief flooded through me. The One-That-Removed, the consumer of too-small flesh, was in time. Where one appeared, more would soon follow. Everything was as it needed to be. All-That-We-Knew would continue to be All-That-We-Know.

Then, joy transformed into horror, my cousins. The human acted according to their nature.

* * *

"We can't let them die — they're intelligent creatures," Susie insisted.

The thing that had stumbled from the cave was five-legged like the Artists but far, far larger. Again, like the Artists, it possessed a long, sinuous neck terminating in a mouth. However, in place of a flat, wide opening filled with molars for grinding plants, this beast's maw was a pit lined with rows of pointed, serrated teeth. Exoplanet or not, Susie was certain this creature ate meat.

The Artists weren't moving. She assumed they were frozen with fear — a reaction she had no difficulty understanding. The carnivore was massive enough to consume an Artist in only two or three bites. It became obvious what would happen if she and Devron stood by and did nothing.

"What do you suggest we —" Devron began.

He paused when the monster lunged and tore the nearest herbivore in half.

Susie drew her pistol and shot it dead.

The sound of the gun echoed in the steep valley.

"I couldn't — I mean, it's not right. I couldn't stand by —" she stammered. "They're intelligent beings."

Intelligent life was so *rare*.

Another predator emerged from the opening in the rock face. A third one followed. Then, a fourth. Another two staggered from the darkness. Yet more lumbered in their wake, growing too numerous to count.

"They heard the gunshot," Devron said.

How like him to apportion blame on her. Susie swallowed a retort as the creatures stumbled in their direction. The predators grew less disorientated. It occurred to Susie they were shrugging off a form of hibernation.

"What's done is done," she finally said. "Rip into me later for disregarding the manual if you want. Doesn't change the fact we're on the menu now. We've got to drive them back."

She took aim and blasted another creature. More reinforcements stepped out from cave mouths that Susie hadn't noticed before. Instead of falling back in panic, the carnivores surged forward, reacting to the volley as if it were a dinner bell. For a second she froze, her mind unable to process anything except the horror of the snarling pack thundering closer.

"Keep firing!" Devron yelled, in what struck Susie as spectacularly redundant fashion. Still, it snapped her out of her shock.

Seeing him rake the predators with a burst from his gun, Susie aimed to the right, targeting a group that had broken off from the main cluster. There had to be nearly a hundred carnivores hurtling their way. They'd brought down twenty, maybe twenty-five. Too hard to tell. Plenty were left, though, and they were too close now, barely a few meters away.

Susie blasted one as it pounced. She must have struck a vital organ because it collapsed to the stony ground, almost close enough to touch.

"We can't hold this position."

One would eventually get through. Like it or not, they were going to have to fall back.

What was wrong with the aliens they'd befriended? Didn't they understand the danger facing them? Panic was well and good — she wasn't immune to it herself — but enough was enough.

Bewildered by their lack of response, she screamed at the Artist clan.

"Run!" Susie shouted. "For God's sake, save yourselves!"

"They're not going to run," Devron spat. "Too stupid or too scared. Hardly matters either way."

He spoke a command into his omni, and a swarm of aerial drones descended on the predators.

"I won't risk retreating. Too likely to get torn to pieces when my back's turned."

Each drone targeted a carnivore and delivered a massive charge of electricity. The attack burned out every one of the local reconnaissance units. But he'd succeeded. The attacking creatures were incinerated.

Susie stared at thin tendrils of smoke curling into the sky. None were left alive. Between the shooting and the drones, they'd killed every last one. She felt weird, being proud of such slaughter — yet she'd saved the Artists. That was worth spilling an ocean of blood. Nothing mattered more than saving them.

Devron broke the ensuing silence.

"Booyah!" he exclaimed. "Humans one, aliens zero. What, you think we'd cross a thousand light years without bringing a means of kicking ass?"

Susie turned at a sound. The Artist with the twisted rear leg was skittering down the last slope of the ridge to her left.

"Come to thank us?" she asked.

Sometimes, despite her species' many flaws, Susie was proud to be human.

The translation came from her omni.

"Why? Why have you done this?" the herbivore asked. "Why have you murdered us?"

* * *

The human did not understand, of course. What they thought was kindness was cruelty. What they assumed was heroism was genocide.

Cousins, I tried to explain. I begged for the human to find and bring more meat-eaters to us before hope was lost. They did not listen.

Around us, the clan died. Not all at once, not mercifully. Death came crawling, hesitant, lingering; it claimed the clan one by one until, after many long fractions of the day, all were gone.

Every ten warm seasons, I told the human, we must seek out the creatures that consume. Our pods grow too large for our chests and must be removed from our bodies. If this release is not achieved, the pods perish. They die from constriction and lack of the substances needed to trigger the next phase.

The meat-eaters perform this task for us. They are not our enemies. We live in harmony and have since the earliest ages of the world. Our forms sustain those who consume us. In turn, our pods are swallowed, their exteriors cleansed in the stomachs of the Ones-That-Remove-Bodies, and then, undigested, are gently deposited on the thawing slopes of the sunlit mountain valley.

There, the Sayer stands guard over burgeoning pods, as the carnivores rest and digest their feast. Pods ripen, prompted by vapors in

126

sunbaked scat, and new bodies form about the pods. The pods, in turn, shrink as they exhaust their reserves, becoming brains in those new bodies; brains that contain the uninterrupted consciousnesses of the clan. The brains grow nerves that link to tiny, new-grown pods in the underside of each clansperson; pods that slowly take up equal part in who each clansperson is, so the cycle of rejuvenation can begin anew.

Legs weak with new growth, the clanspeople arise, clad in young flesh, and the Sayer croons to them of All-That-We-Know, so they remember who they were before they slept.

And once the clan can walk, the Sayer leads them back to our ancestral lands and adds a fresh mark upon the Great Tally and silently rests in their midst and, body exhausted beyond its uttermost reserves, slips, content, into the eternal nothingness of death, satisfied the clan continues and grows slowly in numbers from the rare spawning of double pods, and only the Sayer is lost.

This, I told the human.

"Cut free the pods," came their reply, at last.

The human lives to debate, to believe it knows best.

"A pod can only grow new flesh once cleansed," I repeated.

"We can clean the pods with means unknown to you," they claimed. "High above is that-which-brought-us. Its body contains many mysteries."

"Can you perform these miracles before the cooling of this day?"

They could not, they admitted.

More words came. They protested that they could not have known. They were experts at meeting new life and nurturing it. They insisted there was no possible way they could have anticipated that letting the clan 'die' was the only way it could live. It went, they said, against all possible logic.

Calming, perhaps knowing their thoughts were devoid of truth, they offered to speak with more of their kind. Wise human Almost-Sayers, who might conceive of methods to yet save the clan.

"No," I said, for their words were the babblings of fever-struck fools. "You have ended the clan. I shall end you."

I killed them there in the high mountain pass. Their sprites were dead, unable to save the humans. I had sensed the sticks that caused destruction from afar, so I kicked them from the grasps of the human, and then I trampled the monsters into the mountain's hard stone.

But hear me cousins. Hear me well.

More humans exist. As many as us, perhaps. They believe they are right. They believe they are just. They will return, in greater numbers, to save us. Cousins, they will end us all with their compassion.

Hear me well when I say this: Fear the human — and kill it on sight.

Mike Morgan was born in London, but not in any of the interesting parts. He moved to Japan at the age of 30 and lived there for many years. Nowadays, he's based in Iowa, and enjoys family life with his wife and two young children. If you like his writing, be sure to check out his website: Perpetual StateofMildPanic.wordpress.com and find him on Bluesky (culttvmike.bs ky.social) as well. Mike has published more than 70 short stories with his works appearing in Flame Tree, Best of British Science Fiction, Utopia Sci-Fi, Haven Spec, and other notable publications.

VII

Not James

By: K.L. Mill

Not James

Sophie squinted in the shed's dim light, watching James fiddle with the ancient radio. Dust motes danced in the gleam of the lone bulb swinging overhead, the air thick with the scent of oil and old hay.

"Come on, James." Sophie sighed, shifting against the wall. "I'm bored. And you're never going to get that thing to work."

"Oh, ye of little faith." James flashed a grin at his sister. At fifteen, he was all elbows and knees. He had also convinced himself he could talk to aliens with a ham radio. "There's a meteor shower tonight. If I can just tune in to the right frequency …"

"Hook your ears up to it — you'd get great reception."

Sophie ducked, and an old rag hit the wall behind her.

She turned over a milk pail and sat down.

"You know, Travis Baumgartner says his cousin works at NASA, and he says there's no way a ham radio could intercept alien broadcast. He says anything you hear on the radio is just satellite interference."

James snorted and shook his head.

"Travis also said his grandfather went on tour with the Beatles. Travis is a moron."

Before Sophie could find something to chuck back at her brother, static crackled through the radio's speakers, punctuated by bursts of garbled voices. James's eyes lit up — he grabbed the hand-held microphone right as a screech of feedback pierced the room. The children doubled over, clutching their ears. Tremors rocked Sophie in her feet first; soon the entire building was juddering like a rocket booster during lift-off. White light pulsed slowly through cracks in the shed wall.

"James? What —"

Sophie's voice cut off as a sharp beam of impossibly bright blue-white light lanced through the roof. It engulfed James, lifting him off the ground; his eyes widened, mouth gaped in a silent scream.

For a heartbeat, Sophie saw every detail with crystal clarity: the freckles on her brother's nose, the hole in his left sneaker, the way his hair stood on end. Then the light blinked out.

James was gone, leaving only the fading static from the radio.

Breathing raggedly, Sophie took one tentative step forward, then everything melted into gray.

* * *

Sophie's eyes fluttered open. The bright yellow walls of her bedroom had replaced the shed. Gauzy curtains billowed with the breeze. Her worried parents hovered beside her bed.

Her tongue felt thick, her thoughts sluggish.

"James …" she mumbled. "The light …"

Her mother's face crumpled.

"Oh, sweetie. You hit your head pretty hard when you passed out. And James wasn't there. We – we can't find him …"

Conversations were held in hushed tones in the corner of her room, but Sophie eventually pieced together that almost two days had passed since the events in the shed. James's disappearance was front page news. Her mother fussed over Sophie, changing the bandage on her head with tenderness, but her eyes were flat and distant with worry. Sophie tried several times to tell her parents what happened, specifically about the light that took James, but they only reminded her that a concussion could have lasting effects.

Officer Ferris visited every other day, filling his notebook with details that seemed irrelevant to Sophie. He kept asking the wrong questions.

Did James have any enemies?

Had he been acting strange?

Did he have a girlfriend?

She wanted to smack the notebook out of his hand. None of those details mattered. The light had taken him.

Sophie confronted Officer Ferris one evening while he sipped coffee at their kitchen table.

"The shed," she insisted. "Has anyone checked the radio in the shed?"

Her father and the officer exchanged glances.

"Sweetheart," her dad said gently, "Nothing was in the shed. The radio was just sitting there, unplugged. It hasn't worked in years."

Sophie stormed off to her room, frustrated that no one would listen to her.

The next few months were a blur. Flyers with James's face appeared on every telephone pole and in every store window. Police cars patrolled the streets at all hours. A community search party combed the woods and fields every Saturday for six weeks, looking for him, until even the most dedicated volunteers stopped showing up.

Sophie overheard fragments of troubling adult conversations during this time:

"…random kidnapping…"

"…no leads…"

"…poor Sophie, so tragic…"

But she knew the truth, even if nobody believed her.

Seasons changed. Leaves fell. Sophie's twelfth birthday passed with subdued celebration. Her mother joined a support group for parents of missing children. Her father started drinking in the evenings, just a couple of beers at first, then more.

And still, no James.

Then, one early October night, Sophie bolted upright in bed. Something had woken her – a sound, a feeling, she wasn't sure. The old farmhouse creaked around her; it felt strangely alive, a barely perceptible humming emanated from the walls, vibrating deep in Sophie's bones.

Then she saw it.

Light, brilliant, streaming through the gap under her bedroom door. Sophie crept across the worn wooden floor. Her hand trembled as she reached for the knob.

The door flew open.

James stood in the hallway, backlit by an impossibly bright light. His body swayed; then, like a marionette whose strings were cut, he crumpled to the ground and the light vanished.

Sophie ran to her brother and cradled his head.

"Sophie," James said, his voice a croak. "I'm home."

* * *

Everyone called it a miracle. The kidnapping case revived briefly, but James said he remembered nothing about his abduction. Doctors chalked it up to trauma. As the weeks passed by after his return, the initial flurry of concern and curiosity faded. Whispered theories turned to casual gossip while the rhythm of small-town life slowly returned.

But things were far from being normal again.

The first time Sophie saw James standing in the cornfield at 3 AM, she blew it off. Who wouldn't have trouble sleeping after everything

James had gone through? Her feelings changed when, night after night, she'd look out her window and find him motionless. His silhouette stood stark against the moonlit stalks, his head tilted to the sky.

On the third night, Sophie wrapped herself in a sweater and followed him. Cornstalks crackled as she stepped over dry husks, the soil cold beneath her bare feet. James didn't seem to notice her approach.

"Hey," she whispered, when she was just a few feet away.

James turned slowly. In the moonlight, his face looked hollow, his eyes too large.

"They're coming back," he said flatly.

"Who?"

"The others." He looked up again, scanning the endless canvas of stars. "I need to be ready."

Sophie shivered, but not from the cold.

"Let's go back inside," she urged, taking his limp hand.

To her relief, he followed.

Life settled into a new kind of routine, punctuated off and on by her brother's odd behaviors that everyone except Sophie largely ignored. One night after dinner, James did something that filled Sophie with dread.

He refused a slice of peach pie.

His mother froze with the pie server hovered over his plate — you'd have thought he slapped her face.

"No pie?" she verified.

"No, thanks, Ma, I got an essay to write."

With that, James excused himself from the table.

Sophie watched him lope up the stairs. James loved peach pie, to the point he'd sometimes make himself sick eating too much. Now he suddenly had no interest in even one slice.

Sophie shuddered, knowing deep down that James wasn't really James anymore.

Another clue? Since returning home, he went from C's to straight A's in his physics class.

The scratching clinched it. Hardly noticeable at first, James would absent-mindedly scratch the back of his neck — while doing homework or watching TV … always the same spot.

All these oddities had to be connected to the abduction.

One Saturday, Sophie found James back in the shed, hunched over the old ham radio. His fingers moved with uncanny precision, adjusting knobs and wires. A low humming pulsed above the ever-present static.

"Hey —" She leaned against the doorframe. "What are you up to?"

James looked up from the radio.

"Just fixing this old thing." He grinned. "Remember how we used to listen for alien broadcasts?"

Sophie's heart clenched.

"Yeah," she said, moving closer. "Good times."

James returned his gaze to the radio, completely absorbed. Sophie stepped behind him.

"So, how does this part work?" she asked, pointing over his shoulder at a random component.

As James leaned forward to explain, Sophie studied the nape of his neck. There, barely visible beneath his hairline, was a small, perfectly circular mark, raised in the flesh.

It pulsed with a faint, bluish light.

* * *

Sophie sat on the porch swing, gently rocking in crisp air as the sun dipped below the cornfields. Inside, she heard muffled sounds of her family preparing dinner: her mother's laugh, her dad's low rumble, and Not James sounding so perfectly like himself it made her chest ache.

She knew she should tell her parents about the mark on James's neck … but really, what was the point now? And honestly, it didn't seem that important anymore, for some reason.

Her mother's voice floated through the screen door.

"Soph? Dinner!"

"Coming."

As she stood up to go inside, her gaze was drawn skyward. The first stars were glimmering in the gathering twilight, brilliant pinholes in the darkening fabric of the universe. They were mesmerizingly beautiful.

Sophie's hand drifted to the back of her neck, absently scratching an itch, as she watched the night sky deepen.

K. L. Mill's Midwest roots are so strong, she lives in the house she grew up in that her father designed. She's also a voice actor (another vocation that revolves around words), and when she's not talking to herself in her padded room (home studio), she tries to get the voices out of her head and onto the page. She will read anything in the horror genre but prefers to write fiction that's short and a little strange. Like herself. Most recently, her work has been published by Small Wonders, Cursed Morsels and Crepuscular Magazine; she also has stories included in the anthologies Greater Than His Nature (Atomic Carnival) and Once Upon a Future Time, Vol 4 (Brothers Uber).

VIII

Space Amoebas

By: David Castlewitz

Space Amoebas

Audrey thought she still had time to become famous. She passed the pinnacle of her career as an exobiologist long before she turned 85; but she knew she had something great to contribute. She just hadn't yet figured out what that "something" might be.

Studying her favorite suit in her cabin's full-length mirror, Audrey appreciated how much it flattered her surgically repaired figure. She could've also paid for real hair to cap her bald head, to go along with de-aging procedures done on the rest of her body, but she had grown to like the bare look and didn't want to part with her wig collection. Tonight, she chose a red pixie cut. It resembled her real hair, which flowed down to her waist when she was young.

Low on funds, Audrey hadn't leased a sleeper pod for the long trip from Far Station Neptune One to Mars. Even with a jump-gate, the voyage would take close to a year to complete. To offset the expense, she offered to hold occasional lectures on her life's work. Her audience would be miners and business types, plus tourists who also traveled cheaply. Would they appreciate what she had to say? She prepared herself to be heckled and knew some in the audience might fall asleep.

Audrey just hoped no one brought up "space amoebas."

With her favorite suit's color tag set to yellow, she left her cabin and flagged down a guide-bot to take her to deck five. Once there,

Audrey pulled her waist-length jacket tight, raised her dimpled chin, and strolled into the lecture hall. Only a handful of travelers were scattered about in the large auditorium.

A few people snored in padded recliners. They had to be miners, she thought, based on the rough cut of their clothes. Others in the room were young, so she pegged these as students. A few older men and women perked up, ceased their conversations, and gave Audrey their attention when she mounted the stage.

The lights dimmed. Only a spotlight remained, and it fell on her. She sucked in a deep breath, ready to start. didn't need notes or a teleprompter. She could talk about alien life for hours unaided, her discourse as varied and mysterious as life itself.

"What about those space amoebas?"

Naturally, the first question from the audience was the one she dreaded.

"Yes. How about those things?" She laughed, brushing off the would-be heckler. "They're not amoebas. They may not even be alive. But they are not the subject of my talk."

"Didn't you go to that space station to study them?"

Had she?

So much time had passed since she set out to examine this space phenomena that Audrey had forgotten her original motivation. The lifeform only fed the public's imagination because some pundit labeled it with an unrelated misnomer. As she'd explained many times before, the mass outside Far Station Neptune One did not house sentient creatures, amoebas or otherwise, and was no more alive than space rocks.

"Has the government told you not to divulge what you learned?"

The original questioner had a follow-up query.

"See me after class and we'll discuss it," she said.

Audrey's response prompted a round of titters. When the room quieted, she launched into the lecture she planned to give about Dr. Kohl and his abortive search for non-carbon-based life on Mars.

* * *

"Hope I didn't throw you."

Audrey recognized the voice as belonging to the same man who brought up the "amoebas" during her lecture. Her eyes settled on the rough faced man approaching her and she glared at him. He walked with hands jammed in the pockets of his baggy pants, his bare feet tucked into sandals, a loose flowery shirt framing his torso.

The stranger smiled, which gave his craggy face a glimmer of warmth.

"Brad Westerling. Call me Wes."

He extended his hand, palm up. She placed her hand atop his, though for only a moment, just long enough to be polite.

"Did you listen to my lecture?"

Wes shrugged.

"I knew about Kohl. I interviewed him once."

That put his age somewhere past sixty. So, Wes wasn't as young as he looked, Audrey thought.

"I should warn you," she said. "I'm not the authority about what's floating in Neptune's near space."

"I know."

"What's your interest?"

"Have a drink with me and I'll tell you."

She followed him to the door, then out into the corridor, and felt disappointed when he took her to a passengers' lounge called Station 5 instead of his cabin. When Wes picked out a small round table with a red-and-white checkered tablecloth, she noticed it sat in a far corner, away from everyone.

A bot brought them a selection of juices, fizzy waters, and alcoholic additives. Wes picked out a beer. Audrey took a tall glass of straight-up vodka.

"Okay," she prompted. "We're drinking. Now tell me."

Wes stretched his long legs out at an angle from the table. He sipped the golden liquid in his glass, a smile tugging at the corners of his wide mouth.

"I'm a journalist," he said.

"What's that have to do with anything?"

"I'm not an academic. I think that's —"

"Not important."

"Right to business? No preamble?"

"Is this business? You said you have an interest in the — the things near Station One."

"Yes." He took a deep breath. "I don't know what they are, but I can tell you what they are not."

Audrey shrugged, fast losing interest in this stranger.

"You didn't get very far investigating them, did you?" he asked.

"That's right."

Being reminded that she'd struck out when applying for a permit to study the rocks up close didn't endear Wes to her. Audrey had applied several times, entered four lotteries for a seat on an explorer-class vessel, but ultimately had to satisfy her investigative interests using data accumulated by others.

"I can arrange for you to check one out at close range."

She chuckled.

"And why am I so honored?"

He laughed with her.

"I know your work. I was in one of your classes on Mars. Alien life has always fascinated me."

"They're just rocks. Don't fool yourself."

"These rocks are something else."

"Space amoebas?"

"You can be sarcastic about it, but they exhibit behaviors — Never mind. Look, as I said, I'm in the media. I flunked out of college, so I didn't pursue what I really wanted to do. Now I'm looking for a story. A big story. With your help, I can make a name. You can make your name. I'm offering to work with you, Professor Steel."

That brought a smile to her lips and a tinge of red to her face. No one called Audrey professor outside school. Even there, she knew, the students had other names reserved for her when they didn't address her directly.

Wes slipped a hand into his pants pocket and brought out a palm-sized package wrapped in shiny foil.

"How'd you get that?" Her voice wavered. If he wasn't a credentialed researcher, he had no right to anything remotely related to aliens.

"I bought it. A legitimate sale. Authorized by Station One."

"That's hard to believe."

Wes unwrapped the object, which proved to be a small and chunky gray rock with hints of crystals across its surface.

"The media has more sway than you think."

"I guess so," she retorted, miffed that she, a researcher, a *professor* of alien life, had failed to obtain an up-close view of the rocks, but Wes easily bought a piece of ... She didn't know what to call them. Amoeba? Artifact? Plain rock?

"Watch," he said. "Rather, listen."

He pulled a metal rod from his shirt pocket and tapped the rock.

"I didn't hear anything."

"You do it."

He handed her the rod. Audrey bounced it against the gray object. Vibrations traveled into her fingers, along with a pleasant sound that filled her ears and brought tears to her eyes.

She dropped the metal rod.

"What's it mean?"

"You're the scientist. You tell me."

Her mind filled with a jumble of thoughts, none coherent. She tried to put them in order.

"Why's the sound only in my head?"

"What did you see?"

Audrey shook her head, picked up the rod, and tapped again. Once more, her fingers tingled, and a metallic sound filled her ears. Tears gathered at the corners of her eyes again.

Wes leaned forward.

"You see nothing, but you hear sound. With me, the reverse."

"What — why did you tap the rock in the first place?"

"It was an accident," he explained. "I have an antique pen. It has a metal barrel, and I was flipping it with my fingers when …"

He trailed off and shrugged.

Okay, Audrey mused silently. Great discoveries sometimes resulted from accidents. She thought of penicillin, Post-it notes from ages ago. The history of chemistry was rife with such things.

"I don't have the ability to learn more," he said. "That's why I thought of you."

"I'd need equipment to make any progress."

She didn't elaborate. She had no idea what she'd need.

"I was hoping you'd have some ideas just by –"

"I've no ideas that make sense. You think this chunk of rock is communicating with you?" She laughed. "I don't know what you expect me to do."

"Hang onto it. When you return to Mars, you can find the facilities you need to work with it. But keep me in the loop. I want a fantastic story to tell."

"If there is one," she said slowly. then added, "It's a generous offer."

She pictured the accolades that would follow if she did discover something.

"A fair offer," Wes agreed. "You do the work, get academic credit, and I get a scoop."

* * *

Waking up provided the only escape. Awake, Audrey sat up in the narrow bed and tried to identify her surroundings. Moments earlier, she'd been trapped inside a crystal cave. The dream faded; reality replaced oblivion. She swiveled and sat on the edge of the bed, her bare feet on the cold floor.

The rock Wes gave her sat alone on a table next to the bed. She stared at its light-reflective surface. Handling the rock enhanced visions of swamps and then deserts and then vast bubbling seas; with her hands touching the rough surface as wavering sound filled her ears.

Audrey dropped the rock back on the table. Quiet returned. Only to be interrupted by a "visitor" announcement along with a blinking blue light above her cabin door. She expected Wes. He must have news related to the rock, she thought. She checked the time. Ship's time read a little past 6 in the morning. Standard time listed N/A.

Draping herself in a red robe, pulling it tight across her belly and adjusting the folds at her chest, Audrey went to the door. Wes wasn't there to greet her, no early morning visit from her newfound friend.

"Nance Jennelli," the woman said. "Ship's security."

She extended a thin hand, which Audrey automatically touched. The stranger's soft dark eyes contrasted sharply with her tough olive skin. Her oval face and prominent cheekbones spoke to Audrey of tranquil nights on pebble-strewn beaches.

She broke eye contact, and the vision faded from her mind.

"Yes? What do you want?"

Jannelli stepped into the cabin, making Audrey move back from the door.

"I have some questions about Westerling. Brad."

"Wes?"

"Did you see him last night?"

Not that it was the ship's business, but she nodded. She answered more questions: when and where.

"Is this just curiosity?" Audrey asked.

She sat on the edge of her bed, annoyed that the sheet drooped to the floor, uncomfortable being naked under her robe. Still, she continued to answer the questions put to her. They'd had a drink in a passenger's lounge. She didn't visit his cabin, and he didn't visit hers.

"So you never saw him… alone?"

"No."

Audrey sighed. At age 85, she remained attractive and alluring, she thought. He should've taken her to his cabin. Studying the security officer, she judged the woman to be 60 or so. Under that padded one-piece uniform, she could be flabby or sculpted, marked with age spots or covered with rejuvenated skin.

"I'll tell you what this is about."

Jennelli reached into a deep side pocket and pulled out a squat black plastic cylinder, which she showed to Audrey like a child revealing a favorite toy.

She moved to the desk, bolted to the wall, set down the cylinder and tapped its top. Instantly, the device projected a scene that spilled across the desk. A figure lay belly-up on the floor, hands at its throat. As the picture sharpened, Audrey recognized Wes, and she shuddered.

"What happened?" she asked, kneeling at the desk and peering closely at the scene of a narrow cabin like her own, sparsely furnished, very utilitarian.

"We run a health check every morning between three and four. Not to be intrusive. Not even to keep tabs on the passengers. If we don't get a life reading — heartbeat, respiration, radiation, that sort of thing, we check in."

"Check in?"

"Your service bot," Jennelli said, nodding towards Audrey's somnolent aide in a corner. "We're not intrusive, just concerned for safety. A lot of times, the cabin is empty, so we locate the occupant later in the day. The embedded card key in the wrist, a charge registered at a lounge or — Well, anyway, we account for everyone who isn't in a sleeper pod."

Audrey barely heard what the security officer said. She kept staring at the image of Wes lying on the floor with his own hands at his throat.

"He strangled himself?" she asked in an incredulous voice.

"I doubt it. Forensics doubts it as well. We think he was fighting off his attacker."

"But never lowered his hands?"

"You were the last person to see him."

Audrey shrugged.

"Do I look like I could strangle a man who's much —"

"No. Looking at you? No, but maybe he told you where he was going or who else he was seeing?"

Audrey saw a black rock on Wes' desk.

"Can you zoom in?"

Jennelli nodded and the image went blurry, then sharpened, exposing Wes' agony; his bulging eyes, his tongue blue and lolling outside his mouth.

"That's one of those rocks," Audrey whispered, pointing at the object on the desk. "He gave me one to study." She moved to the table next to her bed and lifted the rock Wes had given her. "Whoever killed Wes might've been after that rock."

"Why kill him and not take it? And what's so special about it?"

Looking at the rock in her hand, Audrey realized she couldn't answer the questions without handing the rock to Jennelli, tapping it and letting her experience the result.

As she rolled the idea around in her mind, she imagined the killer rooting through the cabin but not knowing what he wanted to find.

"Doesn't look like anyone ransacked the cabin," Jennelli said. "Nothing even touched. We think the service pod spooked him when it woke up to scan the room. He may've realized there'd be video, that he'd be seen."

"Then you know it was 'he' and not 'she'?"

"Working theory. We don't know anything for certain."

* * *

Wes kept a souvenir, Audrey thought. That didn't annoy her. The fact someone would kill him over it was another matter. If that same person knew she also had a piece of "amoeba", would she be a target?

Audrey sat on the edge of her bed, her own rock beside her. Tapping it with her finger didn't produce the harmonic response she experienced before. She needed metal. Scrounging through her carry-on bag, she found the small wooden box storing her keepsakes. She slid the lid off and emptied the contents onto the bed.

Much of what Audrey saved — invitations to speak at a convention, pins, and holo-graph tubes of old friends — were made of plastic. And then there were her class rings, her favorite one fashioned from steel. Engraved on its oval face was the year she finished her doctorate, 252 YI — year of independence.

She slipped it onto her index finger, down to the first knuckle. She mouthed the engraving: 252. The last year of Mars' independence. By the following year, it had joined the Sol Compendium, reuniting with Earth, the Moon, and all the space habitats.

A light tap against the "space amoeba" produced a pleasant chime in her mind. Then came the lights when she tapped harder. Staccato taps produced a symphony of color and sound. She enjoyed the sensations coursing through her body. Wes came to mind, his smile warming her and his eyes absorbing her. What could've been and never was, he seemed to be saying, moving his lips yet making no sound.

If Audrey ever published something about this space rock, she'd dedicate it to his memory. He wanted a story to tell, but now all he'd have is a mention. The thought saddened her. She sat with the rock on her lap and shut her eyes, irritated by the tears leaking from the corners. Wes wasn't anyone to her. Not a lover. Hardly a friend. An acquaintance, nothing more.

She spoke aloud, explaining it to him. In her long life, she'd found it best to establish ground rules with her peers and her students. Everyone had their place, like chess pieces set up on a board, each in their assigned position.

As in her dream, she found herself in a cave full of light, with flickering specks of crystal above and all around. Faces of friends bubbled up from the earthen floor. But their features were indistinct. How did she know they were her friends, her colleagues, and her students?

When Audrey slipped down from the edge of the bed, the vision vanished. The cave went away in a puff. The twinkling crystals winked out. No more friends rose from the floor. She looked around, seeing she had returned to her cabin aboard the cruiser. *Returned.* As if she'd been spirited away.

Be cautious, she told herself. There might be enemies aboard this ship, men — or women — who'd kill for the piece of space rock she had in her possession. What could she do, hide in her cabin? No. Best to deal with them. Like everything else in her life. She confronted peers who disagreed with her. She'd never been afraid of confrontation.

Audrey sat at a corner table, a mirror on the wall aiding her preparations. Now was the time to don a wig, color her sunken cheeks, adorn her eyes, and ready herself to leave the cabin. Sad, yet refusing to shed tears, she strode to the elevator and steeled herself against any sort of attack. She'd show her bravery and walk into the dining room with her chin up.

As she alighted from the elevator, Audrey absorbed odd looks from her fellow passengers, crewmen working in the corridor, and children at play in an artificial park. She passed a window into a lounge reserved for parents to sit and monitor their kids. She saw her reflection. She marveled at the odd woman staring back at her, a woman with a knobby skull and a few strands of gray hair. Large eyes blackened all around, and plump cheeks glowing red, along with a huge painted violet mouth stared at her.

She felt her head. No wig. She touched her lips and looked at her fingertips. They were tinted purple. Audrey stifled her scream, ducked her head, and raced back to the elevator, back to her cabin. She had to hide.

* * *

Audrey opened her eyes and brushed away the crust on her eyelids. She called for lights. Her skirt and blouse lay on the floor. She remembered donning them. With that memory came the startling recall of how she'd looked earlier. Like a clown. She shuddered at the thought.

She glared at the chunk of rock Wes had given her. It lay nestled in the corner of her pillow. She took hold of it, felt the rock's weight in her hands, and studied the glittering surface. For all she knew, every point of light across its face was some form of life.

"Are you doing this to me?" she asked out loud. "Did you kill Wes?"

The cave came alive with twinkling lights. Suddenly. Then the vision vanished. So quickly did it disappear that she doubted it offered a sign of anything more than her tired mind.

A shadowy figure splashed against the closet doors. It, too, dissolved. Shaking herself, mildly slapping her cheeks with both hands, Audrey opened the closet; the sliding door squeaked on its runner. She pulled out a light blue jumpsuit and dressed.

Maybe it's hunger, she reasoned. She needed food. Sugar. Nourishment.

When she made her way to the dining room, Audrey found it much more crowded than usual, with dozens of travelers and off-duty crew members gathered in front of a large monitor attached to one wall. A talking head referenced Neptune One while an animation in a corner of the screen depicted the space station being slowly surrounded by space rock.

"What's happened?" she asked, directing her question to no one in particular.

"Neptune One imploded," came a reply.

Audrey watched while the station was squeezed together. The station's body and outer modules quickly met each other and then burst, spraying debris out into space. According to the talking head, this either resulted from alien attack or natural gravitational forces yet to be understood. If the former, then the first sign of intelligent life had been discovered in the solar system's outer fringes. If the latter, then deep space exploration held more mysteries to be solved.

"The amoebas did it if you ask me," someone remarked.

Audrey looked for the source of that comment. A buzz of conversation erupted. As she lingered in the crowd, she heard the event occurred two standard days earlier. A supply ship witnessed and recorded it, then sent the recording on to the relay station at the nearest jump-gate.

She slumped into a curved plastic chair, her elbows on the tabletop.

Out of the corner of her eye, she saw Jennelli. Audrey called out to her.

"You leave any friends behind back there?" the security officer asked.

Audrey shook her head. She wanted to tell her about the space rock in her cabin and the smaller piece she saw in Wes'. Except it sounded absurd that either one had anything to do with what had happened. She asked about Wes' body.

"SOP calls for an autopsy."

"Are you storing it afterwards?"

Jennelli shook her head.

"We don't have facilities for that. He'll be shot out into space. Why? You have some religious attachment?"

"No, no."

"Because his shipboard profile didn't specify any."

"When's he to be —"

"Not my department. With what happened at Neptune One, we're on alert. In case it is aliens." She snorted. "Not likely."

Audrey thought fast.

"There's something I want from his cabin."

"Too late. It's been cleaned. Cleared out. We're sending that out along with the body."

Audrey tried to control her too fast breathing and keep her wits about her.

"Can I — I put something in his …. casket?"

Again, Jennelli snorted.

"Where do you think you are? Dead get a shroud and that's it. What's your angle here? Some religious things you didn't note in your bio?"

"No, no. I'd feel better if —"

"Besides, it's not up to me. Check with Social. They handle deaths when they occur. Which is basically never. Not good for publicity."

* * *

Back in her cabin, Audrey examined the space rock on her bed. Did it grow in length or breadth? She hefted it in one hand. It didn't feel heavier. Maybe the rock surrounding Neptune One didn't expand. Perhaps more rock — she'd never refer to them as amoebas — simply attached itself to what was already there. At some point, a gigantic mass surrounded the space station, and then it just became a matter of compression.

Waking nightmarish thoughts plagued her. Audrey refused to think the space rock would explode or grow or do anything to harm her. But then she imagined it ballooning in size, forcing walls to buckle and creating havoc for the cruiser. She shook her head to cleanse her mind. She was mature enough, with enough experience in her field, to know what was real and what was true menace.

"Free us," she heard in her head.

When Audrey shut her eyes, she saw the crystals in that cave, but now they had eyes and mouths. Frightened, she opened her eyes and took a deep breath, only to be greeted by that shadow she'd seen earlier. It crawled across the closet doors, elongated nails reaching out from a slimy body.

She ran to the closet and slapped it. The vision vanished, but she now had the urge to rake her face with her own nails. Except they were too short. Audrey felt only the pressure of her fingertips. Her nails didn't draw blood.

She imagined Wes putting his hands to his throat and strangling himself, obeying the edicts of whatever alien entity inhabited the space rock. Audrey sat at the monitor on her desk and asked to be connected to Ship's Services. A face belonging to a weary-eyed man appeared.

"All questions about Nep One —" he began.

"This is about a space burial."

"— should be directed —"

"Space burial," she snapped, cutting him off a second time.

A different face appeared. This one belonged to a pleasant woman, but Audrey quickly realized it was as artificial as the previous one.

"There is one burial scheduled for today," the woman said.

"Westerling? Brad?"

"Burial Authority found on deck eight."

Audrey grabbed the chunk of rock Wes had given her and ran from the cabin. The rock glowed. Her hand warmed. She entered an elevator and rode to deck eight, followed the sign on the wall to Burial Authority, and barged in on a young desk clerk with a closed chute behind him. Several raised buttons ran in a vertical line in the wall. A cardboard box sat on a plastic slab extending out beneath the buttons.

No shrouded body, though.

"Westerling," Audrey said, barely able to breathe at the same time.

"Sorry," the clerk's deep voice didn't match his skinny build. "No one said there'd be anyone saying goodbye."

"You … shot him out?"

Audrey stared at the closed chute. She doubted the clerk would accept the crystal-lined rock and send it into space. Not unless she had a good story to tell him.

"He wanted this to go with him," she lied.

The clerk shook his head, refusing to take the rock from her palm when she tried to hand it over.

"Nothing goes out without authorization. Sorry."

Audrey glanced at the cardboard box.

"His personal effects," The clerk explained before she could ask. "You want a memento?"

She turned to the box, lifted a flap and dropped the rock inside among Wes' belongings. The small crystal-lined specimen he'd kept for himself glowed.

"You sending this out?"

"The box? Yeah. Just getting ready —"

"Do it! Now."

Before the strange crystals took control. She didn't know what they could do, but the sooner they left the cruiser, the safer everyone would be.

"Did you get what you wanted?"

Audrey nodded.

The clerk moved the box across the slab to a spot in front of the chute. From the movement of his arms, she could tell he was rooting through Wes' effects.

She called him on it.

"All part of my job," he replied to her challenge. "In case there's contraband."

"No. In case there's something valuable."

"There isn't. It's already been picked through."

The clerk hit a button. Audrey held her breath, her face reddening. Her stomach churned. The clerk pushed the box through the chute and shut it. He hit another button and a dark monitor in the wall came to life. Audrey watched the box float away. Space rocks broke through the flimsy cardboard. Moments later, the blackness of space filled the screen.

"Good friend?" the clerk asked.

Audrey shrugged.

"We were just getting to know each other."

She turned abruptly and left the room. A sense of relief flooded her mind. She walked light-footed. Audrey realized she'd been trudging through the corridors, bent over, stomach knotting and twisting.

What would those rocks have done to the cruiser if she hadn't set them free?

She returned to her cabin and flopped on the bed. No more dreams of the cave, no twinkling crystals. Too bad Wes had to die. What did the mind-altering aliens plan for her? Death for interfering with their lives? The nightmares, those that came when she slept and those that haunted her when awake, couldn't be their sole punishment.

The bigger penalty, however, would be the one that struck her professional life. There'd be no grand study, no introduction to a new and strange form of alien life. Most likely, the Neptune One remnants would be blasted to oblivion, along with the "amoebas." Most likely, no one would study them. For all she knew, no one would even conclude an alien intelligence brought on the space station's demise.

Something glittering caught her eye. Audrey looked at a tiny shard that twinkled in the overhead lighting. It resembled a fish scale. She gently retrieved it from the table next to her bed, set it onto her fingertip, and marveled at how reflective light played across what was obviously a piece of the alien rock. A piece of crystalline life; hopefully, a piece too tiny to do her harm.

But still big enough to be taken to her lab on Mars.

Audrey retrieved her box of keepsakes and put the translucent shard onto a square of plastic. She sealed the box and put it aside, then toyed with ideas of how to analyze the entity, this "space amoeba."

After retiring from a long and successful career as a software developer and technical architect, David Castlewitz turned to a first love: fiction of all sorts, especially SF and fantasy. Living north of Chicago, David has wonderful winters that keep him inside and splendid (though short) summers for walking, biking, and fishing. All three give him time to contemplate new story ideas. He has published stories in Cosmic Crime, Future Syndicates II, Martian Wave, SciFan, Bonfires and Vanities, and other online and print magazines. Visit David's website, <u>davidsjournal.com</u>, to learn about his past, present, and future stories.

IX

Adaptive Algorithm

By: Charles Chin

Adaptive Algorithm

To the reconnaissance team who finds this letter,

I hope my handwriting is still discernible after being unused all these years. I find the jitter in my wrist makes the strokes uncoordinated, a lingering impact of whispers still in my ear. This is, however, the only way to truly convey my message while still containing this threat and keeping it from reaching the greater Network. It is imperative you follow these instructions and end your search on the planet's surface. But I suppose I should start from the beginning.

The directive files for our mission should still be in the archives. I assume you've reviewed them, but in short, we were tasked with investigating an anomalous report from a deep space probe not seen before. Spectral analysis indicated technology levels on par with interplanetary civilizations: Class A alloy refining techniques, advanced Artificial Intelligence, even basic dark matter reactors. But we found no stellar output: no spacecraft, no space bound signals, not even rudimentary satellites. A curious mix unheard of in all the discovered civilizations throughout the Network.

Upon arrival, we scanned the planet from orbit for twenty standard days. We concluded something fascinating: despite a constant stream of electronic chatter, no intelligent life could be detected. The remnant civilization instead continued as an amalgamation of automated systems, all working together for a people that no longer existed.

We should have left it there. Logged the scans and turned toward the next anomaly in the queue. But our curiosity got the better of us. And why wouldn't it? Is that not why we joined? To find that which has never been found? But I digress.

We set down on the outskirts of the largest city. Settlements and buildings were laid out in a hub and spoke pattern, individual small structures connecting to larger nodes until they agglomerated into huge mega-structures. Quite ingenious, if you think about it. Streamlined travel, simplified logistics. Probably why the entire civilization failed all at once while still leaving the skeleton of automation behind.

We first encountered the Algorithm in an intermediate node between two large housing structures. A rectangular display flickered with bright colors, waves washing together in a rainbow swirl, ever changing. It danced for no one, facing a chair empty of everything save a small metal ring. We thought nothing of it at the time and continued exploring further into the city.

Screens continued to appear, each one awash with a spectrum of color, each a unique pattern of movement. Paired with each screen, a chair with a similar metal ring on the seat, if not close by on the floor. Before long, we discovered an entire district off one spoke, stacks of individual rooms with their own viewing centers. It reminded me of a brig, to be honest, with sterile white walls reflecting colors from the screens like water at night.

Mason interacted with one of the devices first. She placed a probe on a metal ring and spent a cycle attempting to interface with it. I left her to work and took my own scans of adjoining rooms before she called us over, showing her data slab.

A remarkable piece of engineering, those rings. True organic-to-digital bridge devices, capable of reading the consciousness of the wearer and directly interfacing with any linked digital stream. The level of sophistication was extremely advanced, much beyond what the rest of their civilization would have implied. It honestly may have surpassed our current over air methods of computer interface. We chalked the discrepancy up to happenstance, the random noise of an infinite universe.

The first signs that something compromised our systems came at morning meal the next day. Mason had an affinity for a particular classic adaptation of Lady Parnell and the General. She knew every detail of the film, including a scene where a modern speeder races through the rolling hills of ancient Tohm in the background. One of those silly mistakes film aficionados like to point out and trade amongst themselves.

She came to the table perplexed, stating she watched the film last night but noticed irregularities: the speeder had vanished, dialogue changed, the actors were somehow more familiar. She thought little of it, but I — ever the cautious type — asked her to get scanned with Medical. Everything came up clean. With another full day of surveying ahead of us, I tabled the issue.

That night, the crew gathered in the ship's lounge for some music and drinks. Channing claimed rights over song choice — he considered himself quite the curator — much to my aversion. His choices were always so experimental, electronic noise you could barely call music. But around the third song I realized I was nodding along, enjoying the music almost as much as my drink. It felt more soulful this time, melodies flitting into and out of static filled tones like a butterfly.

I asked him when he decided to start playing good music. He looked at me like I was crazy, saying he always played this song when it was his turn at the controls. He pointed out the bass line seemed extra heavy, something he hadn't noticed before. We traded friendly barbs until the words turned hostile. I made the slow realization that I heard something completely different from him.

I ran diagnostics all night, test after test, on both the systems and myself. Every report came up normal, every system green. It made little sense, but every tool we had available said the same thing. And as I worked, I found myself humming the tune from earlier, a melody ingrained into my mind like a lyric from a childhood lullaby.

The next afternoon came unexpectedly, as my alarm never went off. My head pounded as if I spent the night drinking. I stumbled groggily to the mess to find myself alone, nary a crew member in sight. A cursory search found most of the crew either still asleep or watching their bunk screens. Their eyes couldn't be swayed from the displays, locked in place by dazzling images. Even as I tried to grab their attention with waved hands and snaps, they held firm to the lights.

At that moment, I regret I hesitated. They looked so happy and, on those screens, I saw the song in my head, conducted like swaying grass on the edge of a white moor. It beat against my eardrums, pushing into my head with the weight of a thousand trumpets.

Fortunately, I found my footing and forced myself to move, throwing open doors until I found Mason. I pulled her out of her bunk long enough for her to become lucid. She said the Lady Parnell film was different now. All plot inconsistencies had vanished, and the romantic lead now looked exactly like an old college flame of hers. It enraptured her now. I saw it in her eyes and in the way she spoke. She wanted nothing else more than to return to that film, return to a world now tailor-made for her.

I took a boot to her screen. Something had infected us, but with what I still couldn't tell. All I knew was that every video, every song, every piece of equipment with a display could no longer be trusted. The medical scans would be useless, along with any other sensor we tried to run. They'd only report everything was fine.

I felt imminently grateful for having a full view cockpit on the Endeavor. I had to trust my own eyes, hope the physical world still behaved as it should. I took the ship skyward, high enough that I saw the entire city through the ship's transparent bulkhead, silver rods pointed upward like planetary dendrites.

My hands gripped the controls tight, not fighting the ship, but my own impulses. I wanted nothing more than to let go, let the ship coast to the horizon and reach for the dials just to the right. Let myself tune into the song bank and listen to the sweet melody one more time. I almost convinced myself I could do it, just listen for a few seconds and turn it off. Winning that internal argument was one of the toughest fights in my life.

I kept my hands steady, eyes locked on the horizon. I didn't know what I was looking for as I flew, but I knew something out there would help us pinpoint the cause. Call it scientific intuition, or maybe blind hope. After aimlessly wandering for hours, a flash of light caught my eye: a gold-colored dome reflecting the sun, cradled by a small ring of mountains. It sat cut off from other structures as if severed by great tectonic shifts of the crust.

No point in running sensor sweeps any longer. Caution be damned, I set the ship down and stepped out onto soft purple grass. A massive golden doorway lay before me. I pushed hard on the door to reveal a sprawling observatory. Scientific equipment lined the walls, glass shards littering consoles where every display hung smashed to pieces. A makeshift bed lay in the far corner, with signs of survival scattered about the floor.

I stepped closer to find an intact specimen of the people of this planet, half covered by tattered sheets. It lay on the bed, arms crossed over its head, desiccated silver skin pulled tight over thick bones. It must have laid here for years, centuries even, to reach the state I found it in.

I explored the space, pushing aside stacks of papers with symbols I had no hope of deciphering with our compromised translator. My temples pounded as I searched for any clue that would help us fix our ship, and fix ourselves, but my hands came up empty. Close to giving up, I noticed the center of the room had been carefully curated and cleaned, to a much higher degree than the rest of the observatory. Upon further inspection, I found the raised center platform held a telescope reassembled into a rudimentary projector.

I stepped forward and found a large hand crank attached to the floor. With no other option, I spun the handle and forced my way through the inertia of centuries of neglect.

Slowly, gears turned. The teeth of one gear latched onto another, then another, until a symphony of clattering metal filled the room. A light flickered on, powered by my strength, and shot through the machine as clear sapphire panes began dropping through the projector from an overhead hopper. I found myself creating a film thrown onto the dome of the observatory for an audience of one.

A figure appeared, bearing a striking resemblance to the one laid to rest behind me. He made no effort to speak, instead gesturing towards symbols he carved into the metal plates beside him, changing out plates at intervals like he was giving a technical talk. He, too, was a scientist. Don't ask how I knew; we just have a knack for picking each other out of a crowd. I can only guess at the nuances of his presentation, but thankfully the language of mathematics and science tend to be universal.

The people of this world seemed to be much like those in the Network, in the general sense. At some point, they created an Algorithm. Perhaps not a true AI in the technical sense, but intelligent in its own way. It allowed someone to take a video and *adjust* it. Change it enough to make it a little more palatable. Innocuous things at first: remove a blemish, fix a stray hair.

Minor details.

Soon, the Algorithm spread everywhere. People built entire personas based around idealized images of themselves. Soon, the Algorithm was applied to their films. Now, each individual enjoyed a tailor-made movie experience. No more poorly received films, only films guaranteed to please. A person's favorite actor as their favorite character in their favorite genre. Every time.

The changes rippled out. Discourse over films died, and no one shared musical tastes anymore. What's the point in talking about films if no common experience is shared? No overlapping point of discussion? Why share a song when you know the other person hears something completely different?

The alien symbols that flashed before me became too complex to intuit, but I understood the ramifications. No one trusted their eyes or ears. Video evidence, such as security footage, would be worthless. A voice on the other end of the line could be anyone and no one. If the news could *be* anything, how would you *know* anything?

People retreated inwards. The algorithm knew exactly what each person wanted, and made the world look exactly as they wished. It didn't take long for images to optimize themselves until they no longer resembled anything real, just a jumble of colors meant to feed directly into the mind's pleasure centers.

The automations continued their tasks, robotic workers generating power, cleaning floors, maintaining structures, all while the organic population withered and died. Soon, too, their remains were swept up into dust traps of roving machines.

The presentation closed with the alien scientist standing center frame, gesturing with wide arms and mouthing words in a language lost to the stars. Although I could never know the sounds that emanated from his mandibles, I understood the message he imparted.

Do not go down this road.

The delicate clink of sapphire plates fell to silence. I knew then we were a lost cause, infected with a virus we could neither see nor verify. The observatory sat as a mausoleum for an ancient civilization, a warning to travelers to stay away. Unfortunate that we did not stumble upon this place on our first day.

I write what I learned and witnessed so you may know why I had to leave this message in the form I did. No digital hand can corrupt this pen or alter the ink I drive into the fibers of this parchment. I hope this orbital beacon Mason and I cobbled together from scraps can signal you. It's difficult making it complex enough to guide you to our message, but free of any traces of the Algorithm.

Please, don't come to the surface to find us. We've taken great strides in making a life for ourselves here, peaceful ones. We care for the others who are too far gone into their own imaginary worlds, feeding them and keeping them comfortable. Mason still gets the chills sometimes, withdrawal from the screens. I too feel the same pull, an ever-present hand waving me towards that screen of colored lights like a persistent melody in my ear. But we work through long nights together. It's funny how, after all my years, it took me until now to sit down and watch a sunrise.

You reconnaissance teams are mostly military personnel, and you feel the need to save. You hope — you believe — every situation has a solution. But I'm telling you here in no uncertain terms, for the good of the Network, that we must not be rescued. I know the Algorithm now; in the music it sings to me. I can see it as notes on the staff, see how it works. It really isn't that complicated, all things considered. I find it surprising that no civilization in the Network has developed it before. Then again, those who did may invariably end up like the ruined planets that scatter our historical archives.

I can feel it inside my head, pushing me to transcribe it into the Network's language, bit by bit, one line of code at a time. With our technology, we may be able to harness it safely, use it for good. But only a fool would believe that only a good outcome was possible. Even if you retrieve us, and I promise to the Core and the Holy Centris I would never let the secret of the Algorithm leave my lips, I cannot charge the safety of the Network to my strength of will alone. Because one day, that whisper will grow loud enough, and my strength will wane enough to compel my hands to compose a nightmare dressed as a symphony.

So, for the sake of our civilizations, and to respect the one already gone, I bid you farewell and ask you to quarantine this planet forever.

Glory to the Core,
Cal
Chief Science Officer, Science Vessel Endeavor

Charles Chin (he/him) was born in Oak Ridge, Tennessee. Raised by scientist parents to be a scientist himself, he needed a creative outlet to offset the rigid worldview of doctoral degrees and data science. He still writes about science, but on his own terms. Should you come across Charles in the wild, know that he prefers rum over whiskey. Previous stories written by Charles have appeared in Factor Four Magazine, Sunshine Superhighway: Solar Sailings, and Intrepidus Ink.

X

Foreign Exchange

By: Brian Reindel

Foreign Exchange

I stood outside my former home, now owned entirely by my ex-wife, and second-guessed entering unannounced with the spare key. Roxanne asked me to visit and even said to come inside, no need to knock. I still feared the snare of a well-set trap. We were on good terms as of late. I worried it would change based on her tone when she called earlier.

"Hey, anybody home!" I shouted after closing the door behind me.

"Upstairs in Taylor's room!" Roxanne shouted back. "Come up."

I climbed the stairs, cautious, ready for an ambush the moment I reached my son's room. Instead, she stood with her arms crossed, hip bent out slightly, squeezing the anger back in on herself. Whatever happened was obviously my fault and I saw no point arguing. Fighting for dominance repeatedly got me in trouble the last sixteen years. I finally learned my lesson after she served me the divorce papers.

Taylor, my teenage son, sat on the edge of his bed, staring through a window with mama bird hovering close. I couldn't figure out if I was the predator or prey. Roxanne eyed Taylor with compassion, then turned her steely glare back on me.

"Are you going to say something?" Roxanne asked.

"This is a bizarre way to ask for more child support," I said.

"I don't want any more of your money."

"Okay, so what is it then, full custody?"

"This isn't about me, it's about Taylor!"

Roxanne clenched her jaw and ground her teeth. The discussion was headed nowhere fast.

"You call me over here, demanding I take the rest of the day off work and then proceed to tell me our son is possessed," I said. "What did you expect me to think?"

"I didn't know how else to say it. He keeps calling himself by a different name and acting strange. Is it any mystery with all the garbage you exposed him to at an early age?"

The decorations in Taylor's room communicated our shared interest, a sincere bond we developed, but then fractured over recent months. I was surprised he kept the science fiction posters and collectibles around, gifts through the years for birthdays and holidays. It led me to believe his interest had been sincere, not simply a child's desire to solicit the affections of his bum father.

An original *War of the Worlds* poster from the 2005 film featuring Tom Cruise hung adjacent to a replica from the 1953 film. Actors Gene Barry and Ann Robinson embraced as a giant Martian's hand reached down from space through an explosive sunset. A tinge of guilt and nostalgia swept through my bones. I wanted Roxanne to hold me the same way.

Who was I kidding? Those days were long gone.

"Taylor, what's going on?" I asked, subdued, not interested in starting an argument.

He didn't answer.

I had to admit his behavior indifference appeared suspicious. Conflict between Roxanne and I used to send him tearing off to a friend's house, or he stood between us, facing off in my direction. We also had our share of screaming matches, increasing the divide between a father and son, but never once had it triggered meditation.

"Hey, Taylor, look at me," I said.

He turned his head but remained silent.

"Son, what's going on with you?" I asked again.

"While this vessel previously responded to another name, it's preferable you direct your inquiries now to 'Zentari,'" Taylor said.

He played off the act as the perfect straight man, with not a smile or even a smirk. I preferred the attitude, or a tongue lashing about how terrible a dad I had been when he needed me most. Roxanne and I dissolved our relationship out in the open. Instead of shielding Taylor from the destruction, I stepped away to avoid conflict. It's possible he learned to play petty passive aggressive games in retaliation or discovered a creative method for bringing me back into the fold.

Regardless, my frustration grew as Roxanne huffed and rolled her eyes. I leaned over and grabbed Taylor's arm, squeezing to demonstrate the seriousness of the situation.

"That's enough, Taylor," I said, emphasizing each word with an extra sternness. "You're going to talk to your mom like a normal, obnoxious teenager."

Taylor grabbed my hand, wrenched and twisted it with a strength a boy of his size should not possess. It surprised me, and I sank to one knee next to the bed, grimacing. I grabbed his wrist with my other hand, but it wouldn't budge. The force exerted on my hand kept me in place but did not hurt unless I pulled.

"Taylor... let... go."

He turned to Roxanne.

"Let your father go, Taylor!"

He obeyed.

"You've been working out," I said, wringing my hand. Hitting the gym was the only reasonable explanation I could offer, unwilling to entertain any other.

"If we need to send him to a psychiatrist," Roxanne said. "It's coming out of your pocket,'" Roxanne said.

"It's coming out of your pocket if we need to send him to a psychiatrist," Roxanne said.

"Fine, *Zentari*, you want to play those games, then give me a sign you're from another planet," I said.

Roxanne rolled her eyes again, unwilling to play the same game.

"For false messiahs and false prophets will appear and perform great signs and wonders to deceive, if possible, even the elect," Taylor said.

His statement confused me. I had heard it before, somewhere, but couldn't quite place the reference. It didn't align with his embodiment as some sort of alien visitor, offering a different sign that this entire experience was the result of a shattered childhood.

"In case you're wondering, it's from the Bible," Roxanne said. "We've been attending church on Sundays."

"Church, as in Jesus church?" I asked.

"It's been good for him — for us — until now," Roxanne said.

"What is this, some sort of savior complex?" I asked.

"Many of my own will come, exchanging our life force with those of humankind, explorers on a similar plane, seeking to understand the noumena realm from your perspective," Taylor said.

"You mean you want to find God?" I asked.

"Is this unacceptable?" Taylor asked.

I looked over at Roxanne, who was on the verge of tears, and placed my hand on her shoulder, an act of comfort she acknowledged reluctantly.

"It's perfectly acceptable, but you don't need to pretend to get my approval," I said. "Taylor, I haven't been the greatest dad… or husband, but I'm open to religion if it will help you."

This didn't outwardly assure him. He lowered his head.

"We can't begin this way," he said.

Without warning, a musical chimp toy on the dresser clanged its cymbals together, startling me and Roxanne. The prop from

Close Encounters of the Third Kind had no batteries and had been broken for years. Next to it, a toy from the same movie, the "Mod Monster Blushing Frankenstein", sprang to life. It was also previously inoperable and held little more than sentimental value. The toy swayed side-to-side, groaning. Its pants dropped to its ankles and the face lit up, blushing, just as advertised. I wanted to believe I witnessed an elaborate prank. When memorabilia began floating off the shelves, dresser and end table, the truth became undeniably clear.

Roxanne pressed her hands to her mouth and tears streamed down her face. The circumstances revealed an unfortunate outcome; a foreign soul inhabited her son's body, traveling from a distant location, unfamiliar and terrifying. Taylor existed only as a shell. Roxanne turned and tried to run from his presence. Before she reached the door, it slammed shut, eliciting a scream.

The hovering objects settled back down into their place and the toys went silent. Roxanne stepped up close and pressed behind me, partially shielding herself. I welcomed the warmth of her body, a consolation in an impossible situation. We both wanted to know what happened to our son.

"Where is Taylor?" I asked.

"It would be too difficult to explain," Zentari said.

"Try me," I said.

"We are quantum entangled across a vast distance," he explained. "Our consciousness has been exchanged, mine to this physical body, and him to my previous form. While he is unable to respond, our awareness of one another's experiences is mutually understood. Thoughts and feelings are shared simultaneously."

"He's alive?" Roxanne asked.

"Very much so," Zentari said.

"You had no right to do this," she instantly replied. "Bring him back."

"I'm afraid that's not possible. Not yet, anyhow. The exchange is meant to encompass the entire lifetime of a human."

"And you're the first?" I asked.

"Others will arrive, allowing a small group of Earth's inhabitants the opportunity to visit other remote celestial bodies. This has long been a dream of yours, to reach for the stars, to travel among the heavenly hosts in search of life and meaning. We have done it, only sooner."

"Can you choose who?" I asked.

"Yes, every explorer is given the option."

"Then allow me the same choice, as a courtesy," I said. "Take me instead and bring Taylor back to his mother."

Roxanne gripped my arm in desperation, hoping Zentari would agree. It would not correct the poor choices I'd made in the past, but it would give her comfort by eliminating the fear of a future full of unbearable loneliness.

"And what of Taylor, if he is satisfied in his current state?" Zentauri countered. "I sense reluctance, the pain of doubt and the fear of loss. He will experience a greater sense of joy and fulfillment living in the paradise my homeworld provides. Are you willing to take this from him?"

"I can give him something else in return," I said.

"So be it," Zentari said.

Roxanne turned me around and hugged tight around my waist with her head pressed against my chest. She pulled back, kissed me on the cheek, and started to say something when the world turned black.

A chaotic kaleidoscope of shapes and colors stretched out into eternity, like a row of crayons once confined to neat rows, but now succumbing to blistering heat, molten and bleeding together, dissolving into a shimmering landscape. The shapes eventually contracted, forming galaxies as I lingered, floating in the dark abyss at what appeared to be the event horizon of a black hole. I had no physical body, only an awareness of the surroundings.

Another consciousness lingered inside the same space and time, both of us squeezed together in the cosmos. Without words, Taylor and I shared a moment of communication, first his disappointment, resentment, then resignation. I responded with deep apologies, a desire for reconciliation and a promise to be united somehow. It was all I had to offer. I wished I could have done better, and he understood, but we had to take our regrets to separate ends of the universe, carrying a hope that one day we could fully reconcile face-to-face. My travels continued through the black hole, where I circled the drain and shot out the bottom, rocketing to a destination of glowing, golden beauty.

My understanding of this process and my place in the universe was only possible by sharing the knowledge of Zentari. My consciousness existed in his physical form, flying above the surface of a planet with sparkling shores and an expanse of tall, slick buildings dotting the landscape. Their surface moved in waves from top to bottom, and I realized the structures were both practical and organic, living domiciles.

The final exchange had taken place, and my new home called. I would seek answers and one day hoped to return to Taylor. Maybe someday we could share a passion again as father and son — not one made of fantasies, imaginary scenes cast on vinyl screens, but one of time spent among the stars.

Brian Reindel graduated with a journalism degree nearly twenty-five years ago, switched fields during the dot-com boom, and works now as a software architect. He writes speculative short stories on Substack in his spare time and has published two fantasy and science fiction short story collections: The Stars Will Fall and Voices from the Deep.

XI

Raining Cats and Dogs

By: Katherine Kerestman

Raining Cats and Dogs

They fell right in front of me. Thud. Thud. Thud. A white dog with brown spots and two black cats — one with a beige nose and one with a striped tail — plopped right out of the sky and landed on the sidewalk. Hit the cement as softly as if they had been wearing parachutes.

My friend Joyce and I were standing in front of a wine shop, about to go inside to choose a bottle. (No, we had not had any to drink yet). They just came careening down from the sky on a gorgeous, sunny day in May

I did not see an airplane or a helicopter, not even a drone. Where did they come from? I hurried over and checked to see if they were okay. I got down on my knees and spoke softly to the trio. They appeared to be shaken, shivering and cowering, but not aggressive in the least. I let them sniff my hand and made submissive gestures so they would not feel threatened. The dog licked the back of my hand, and the cat with the beige nose started rubbing her head on my knee.

None seemed to be injured.

I called out to Joyce, whose frozen face indicated her mystification, and asked her to phone an animal-loving friend of ours. I hoped that friend, Leslie, would take one of the animals, at least until we got a better handle on the situation.

"Yes, Leslie will take the dog," Joyce said softly, remaining in the shop's doorway to keep from spooking the animals. "Leslie will be here in a few minutes."

All my life I have loved animals, with a special fondness for felines. Cats are naturally quiet and gentle creatures, never vicious except when through experience they have learned fear. And they are dependent upon kind people for their survival.

I sat cross-legged on the sidewalk, cuddling the cat with the striped tail in my lap and stroking her back in an automatic kind of motion, as I pondered how the animals had dropped there.

When the dog started yelping, I clutched the cat protectively with my right hand, and I turned to my left. A scorpion was perched upon the dog's rump!

"It just dropped from the sky!" Joyce exclaimed. "I saw that scorpion fall right out of the sky!"

"Joyce, quick — hurry!" I pointed down the street. "Get a tablecloth from Isabella's. *Hurry!*"

Joyce filched a linen cloth from the wrought-iron enclosed patio of the neighboring restaurant.

Drop it on top of the scorpion and scoop him up in it — Scoop him up *quickly!*" I hissed. "Come at him from behind. *Creep* up on him quietly, Joyce."

Holding her breath, she crept. Stealthily — in a wide arc around our little group on the sidewalk. Except for some surreptitious glances at my friend, I fixed my eyes upon the scorpion, praying the dog would not startle him. Joyce moved quickly. She flung the cloth over the scorpion and ensnared the beast. I moved the cat from my lap and sprang to my feet to assist her with her bundle. We had succeeded! I released my grip on the fabric and faltered back. Where the alley opened next to the wine store, I spied a metal trash container with a lid.

"There," I said, pointing. "Let's put him in there!"

While I lifted the lid, Joyce dropped the bundle into the can. I replaced the lid, pushing it down hard. Joyce picked up some bricks in the alley and piled them on top. We leaned against the fence, wilting.

"Oh, my God!" Joyce cried.

I followed her gaze and saw a green eel slithering toward the dog. I ran toward the eel, stomping my feet. It veered away from the other animals and slithered into the street.

"What was that?" asked Leslie, rolling her window down as she pulled her green Volkswagen up to the curb. "Was that a snake?"

"Something like that," I answered. "Look, come see the dog and cats."

Leslie parked her car and walked over to where Joyce and I were standing.

"Oh, what a cute little puppy, and such pretty kitties," she cooed in a sing-song voice. "How did you get here? Where are your mummies and daddies?"

"They just plopped down from the sky right in front of me."

She shook her head, as if she were listening to a madwoman.

"No kidding," I told her. "They just dropped onto the sidewalk from nowhere."

"You know that's just not possible," she replied.

"Oh, what a dear little puppy," Leslie continued, turning her attention from me to the dog. "I am going to like having him at home. I brought some puppy treats with me."

She gave the dog a handful of kibbles and looked up at us.

"You guys, he's starved! Those cats are scrawny, too. They're all hungry."

"I'll get some food for them at the corner store," Joyce said. "I'll be right back."

She picked up her purse and headed down the street.

"You're right," I told Leslie. "I really hadn't had a chance to notice how thin they are, what with the surprise of them dropping right out of the sky, and then the scorpion and eel …"

"Scorpion!" She gasped. "What scorpion?"

After I filled her in, Joyce returned bearing a bag of cat and dog food along with some paper plates and bowls. She opened the pull-top cans while I took the bowls into the restaurant to fill them with water. When I came back, six more hungry-looking cats and a skeletal dog were sitting in a semicircle watching the other animals eat.

"They're hungry, too!" Leslie exclaimed. "Where did all these hungry critters come from?"

"I rescued two starving stray cats just yesterday," Joyce said. "They were scavenging in the dumpster next to the drugstore. I don't have room for any more now."

"I found three hungry kittens under my car this morning and I took them to the vet," I said. "I'm supposed to call and check on them later."

Both cats were rubbing my legs now, and I picked them up. Leslie knelt by the dog.

"I'll call you Van Helsing," she said scratching his nose, while he licked the plate clean.

"Oh, I guess I'll call the cats Lucy and Mina, then," I said. "I'll just take them home for now, until I find a forever home for them."

"Well, I'll alert the Humane Society about these other critters, and I'll wait here for the agent," said Joyce said. "I'll call you tonight."

"Thanks again, Leslie," I said gratefully. "I just cannot figure out how they dropped right in front of me. And all these other hungry animals, too! I'll talk to you tomorrow."

"You're quite welcome. Van Helsing is so cute! Brian's going to be surprised tonight."

"Not really — he knows how you are."

I smiled and waved goodbye to Joyce and Leslie. I set the cats down to retrieve my handbag, and then I picked them up again and walked to my car.

* * *

Darkness descended early on a late fall afternoon. I had finished washing the dishes and cleaning up the kitchen. The cats were asleep on the sofa. I started packing away the Halloween decorations and carried some boxes to the storage shed. I considered bringing some Christmas decorations back to the house on my return trip, but did not feel ready for Christmas yet. On my way back, a commotion drew my attention, so I walked around the front porch to the far side of the house to see what was happening.

I discovered a dozen assorted canine and feline guests assembled at the back door as if waiting for their dinners. Hearing a thump, and a clatter, I turned and saw two dogs dropping from the sky onto into the wheelbarrow, still in the same place I'd left it when I cleaned out the flower beds the day before. I looked up, of course, but only saw a little moonglow behind a lot of grey clouds. It was so dark a dirigible could have been up there, and I wouldn't have known it. I went inside for paper plates and a couple of bags of cat and dog chow. After I fed the ravenous crew, I called the Humane Society to come for the orphans, since my own ark was full.

When George, one of their agents arrived, his eyes widened like saucers at seeing all the animals.

"Where'd these all come from, Angelique?" he asked.

"They just dropped from the sky," I said, spreading my arms in wonder.

"Now, come on, where did they really come from?" he replied, leaning against his truck.

A groundhog dropped onto the hood of his truck. Plunked right by his elbow.

"God!" George flinched. What's that?"

"A groundhog."

"Where'd it come from?"

"The sky."

"You know better than that."

"All right, then you tell me," I said.

George rubbed his fingers in his hair and shrugged.

"Help me load these guys up in the truck, Okay?"

"Okay."

* * *

After a breakfast of coffee and toast, I put on my coat to leave for work. It was still dark outside when I locked the door and walked to my car to leave for work. The days are so short at this time of the year, like a body shortened by beheading it and cutting off its feet. I got inside the car, started the ignition, put the car in gear – and then hit the brake. Two goats and a horse were standing in front of my car.

I did not have goats or horses.

I drove around them and went to work. The staff was thin. Half the employees had called off; they said they were not feeling well. At lunch, I had a difficult time finding an open coffee shop; most had *closed* signs on the doors. On the way home, I turned on the radio in the car. The newscaster just kept talking about mass migrations of people and natural disasters like drought and flooding. He sounded nervous as he talked as if he silently believed these things were all connected. I stopped for a red light at an intersection, and saw cats scratching at front doors, and dogs sitting on their haunches on porch stoops.

I did not see any people.

* * *

"What's the next thing you remember?"

"Let me think. It seems so long ago. Can we dim this light, or turn it away from my face a little?"

"How's that?"

"It's better. Well, let me think. Yes, as the days went on, I saw fewer and fewer people. I was unable to reach Leslie or Joyce on the phone, after a while. They were not home when I drove to their houses. One day, I went to work and could not get in – the door was locked. I walked around the block, and all the businesses were shut up. On my way home, I stopped at the home of the Andersons, the old couple who were my neighbors, and I found them dead in their rocking chairs on their back porch. They were both up there, in years, though, so it was not really shocking. A sheep and a ferret dropped from the sky right in front of their porch when I was leaving."

"What did you do then?"

"I went home, and I stayed home, after that."

* * *

The man in the blue uniform drove me home in a black car, as was our custom. He opened the door for me, with a quiet smile and a nod, and I went into my house. One result of the current circumstances meant I had to manage a larger household than I preferred. I set out several China bowls filled with cuisine for my cats and assorted house guests, before I prepared my own dinner. After that, I nestled into a comfortable chintz chair with a cup of tea and a Victorian novel, and a cat on my lap. The driver would be coming back for me in the morning. He said they are interviewing the people that are still here. Many have died, he said, and many more have run away. Occasionally, another animal drops from the sky. There are a lot of domesticated animals in need of care, he said.

"There's another strange angle," My driver told me as he brought me home from the federal office building, where they had been interviewing. "It's raining like monsoon season, but in the deserts. The rain is pretty much non-stop and heavy. It's spreading from the Middle East and Africa and moving westward across the globe. People are dropping like flies, some of them from unknown causes. Many are fleeing to drier parts or just running ahead of the rain. RVs and cars are caravanning the freeways. Many animals, too, especially cats and dogs, are migrating westward, ahead of the storms."

The stories he shared reminded me of Noah. Was another great flood coming? Would Kansas be the new ark?

Maybe I should be packing up my menagerie and moving west, too.

There was no rain here, in Kansas, yet. We had been having a relatively dry year, in fact. A few months ago, I made another expedition to Leslie's house, and this time I found her note. It appeared that she and Brian had gathered their animals and hit the road. They did not have any kind of plan, she wrote in her note, which she assumed her friends would find when they came to look for her. They thought they would go simply because everyone else was going.

***

I made my final expedition to Leslie's house two or three months, I think, after our meeting at the wine store downtown. With no radio, television, telephone, or internet, all I had was a calendar to cross off the days. It is funny that while there was still electricity, like everyone else, I stocked up on groceries. The shelves in the stores were cleaned off in the first few weeks. At first, I drove around, looking at all the empty buildings, wondering where everyone else had gone. The few people I ran into had the same question. The only real information available suggested everyone was heading west — they seemed to catch the idea from each other. I mean, when I asked people, no one ever said *why* they were leaving town.

They just told me they were heading west.

* * *

"Miss ... what can you tell us about the weeks or months preceding this exodus of people?"

"Well, you know about the increase in stray animals — I swear, they seemed to zero in on my place, sort of congregated there. And they dropped from the sky, too, on occasion. No one wanted to believe that, though, and they made up all kinds of excuses. The vets and the animal shelters were overrun with stray animals brought in by concerned people. My own cats stayed closer to home than they usually did.

"There was a drought that summer. There were dust clouds. Temperatures were way above average. We had sporadic communication issues and electricity failures. Water mains broke down — people said the infrastructure was aging — and people started hoarding water, and toilet paper. Then we had a small earthquake, and a dust storm.

"I remember seeing a train, a long one, several miles long, carrying mottled beige and brown camouflage military vehicles — tanks, and trucks, and other things. It was headed west.

"A lot of people decided to relocate at that time. Statements from city hall said that relocation did not make sense. Utility issues and earthquakes are problems that occur from time to time, most everywhere. The motels were doing great business — people from the east were passing through here, going west. They had experienced similar issues at their homes.

"I can't think of anything else to tell you now."

* * *

I did not feel like cleaning up leaves. Usually, I had them all raked up before the first significant snow, so I would not have a soggy mess to deal with in the spring. This year, I limited myself to picking up branches that would hinder lawn mowing, in case I would still be here in the spring to perform that chore. So, after I gave my menagerie their dinner, I took a cold bottle of wine and a glass out to the porch to enjoy the autumn sunset.

I did not sit down on my wicker chair. I did, however, place the bottle and glass upon the wicker table. And then I took in the sight of five or six or seven hundred birds — crows, robins, blue jays, hummingbirds — huddled beneath the roof of my wrap-around porch. Why my house? Why me? Why at all? The purple of the sunset was creeping up from the horizon of a clear blue sky. The hot night air was still. No signs of a storm coming, which would have prompted the flocks to seek shelter. I took myself and the wine back inside, and I huddled inside a Victorian novel, the wine and the sunset forgotten. I could not help thinking about Joyce, though. I had lost track of her late summer, or was it September? She must have gone west too — or somewhere else. I do not know why she didn't contact me, let me know about her plans. Things were not adding up. So, I stayed close to home, always wondering if I should go, too.

But where?

* * *

One day at noon the skies turned from dull autumn blue to slate -like grey. The wind turned cold and gathered force. Great clouds skidded in from the east, nature's dirty wads of dryer lint that mucked up the clean blue sky. I hoped they would keep on moving, past the horizon, to someplace else, but they stationed themselves over my head and turned my life dark. As rolling thunder vibrated the earth beneath my feet, I herded my cats and dogs into the garage, the shed, and the house.

I had barely rounded up the last beast when an especially vociferous kaboom announced the rain.

Rain pounded the roof, clobbering the shingles. I saw nothing beyond the windows except torrents of water. While lightning illuminated the sky, the television turned itself on. A preacher talked about the end of days. No, he was ranting. He alternately raised his fist and pounded it upon the podium. He referenced the Great Flood. I must say, I felt like Noah, with all these critters in my ark. Not a great variety of species were represented here, though. The preacher, wearing a black garment like a choir gown, screamed that the human race was on its way out. It was curtains for us. Annihilation by drowning. I tried changing the station — but his broadcast was shown on every station that came in. I tried the phone, but it was still out. One-way communication between the preacher and myself was all I would get right now.

I turned the TV off and went to bed early.

* * *

"Did you ever see any of your friends, any other people at all, after that?"

"Yes. I went driving around town, I did not dare go too far, though, not knowing what was really going on. A couple of times I met other people out doing the same. A few said they were moving west, fleeing some unknown thing. No one stayed long to talk — everyone only had questions, no information to share. We had stayed long after the majority had gone, we were the ones who did not want to leave our homes or businesses.

"One day I heard a banging on the door. I doubted my senses. The rain and thunder were continuing. No one had come to my house for a long time. I answered the door — it was Joyce! She poured in through the door, and I hugged her hard. She said she had been to Colorado with her parents, and a lot of cats and dogs in their RV:

'Nothing was different there than here,' she said. 'My folks decided to head toward the coast, but I decided to come back. I wanted to look after my place, and I figured you would be here, too. I tried calling you, but our phones and laptops weren't working.'

"Joyce and I opened a bottle of peach brandy and poured tall ones over ice. We shared our mutual bewilderment. I mean, we saw people leaving, we heard lots of rain was coming our way — and had precious little news besides that. Joyce had not seen the deranged preacher, and when I tried to turn the TV back on, it would not work. We could not watch the evening news for continuing coverage of whatever-it-was, not even the doomsday prophet. I made some spaghetti, more for something to do, and we ate. Our conversation ended after a while, as there really wasn't anything else to say.

"After dinner, she went home. She said she would be back for lunch the next day. I never saw her or her car again."

* * *

I grew worried when Joyce failed to return by dinnertime the day after her visit. I donned my coat and galoshes and made a dash for the car. About all I saw in the downpour, on the drive to Joyce's home, were the headlights of a few other vehicles. I pulled into her driveway and tried all the doors and windows, but no one answered, and they were all locked. Her car was not there. I fixed a note to the front door, trying to place the note where it would get the least wet, and I returned home. As I approached the front porch of my house, before I even opened the door, I heard the evangelist of death fulminating on the destruction that was at hand.

The TV must have turned itself back on.

* * *

At the close of yesterday's interrogation at the federal building, the man in the blue uniform returned me to my house, as before. Once inside, I placed a bowl of soup in the microwave and dashed outside into the rain, to tend to my four-legged guests in the outbuildings while my meal cooked. As the animals gathered around me, I endeavored to dish out love and affection in equal measures with the food. The poor things were as frightened as I was.

As I started to leave the garage, a loud noise startled me. I crept to the door, cracking it open and peeking through the crevice. The din seemed to be coming from the house. It was louder than the now-monotonous thunder. I soon realized the voice of the television doomsayer boomed from the house. The whirring of the air itself, humming with a strangely melodic electricity, seemed to enhance his ranting. The windows of the house were aglow with a soft purple, or lavender, light that also illuminated the surrounding area.

Feeling faint with terror, I closed the door and leaned upon it. Swirling, opaque sensations that inhibited rational thought filled my head. I looked for a weapon and picked up a hammer. I carried it on wobbly legs to the house, where the crow-like preacher's ravings poured through the closed door onto the porch. I steeled myself, turned the doorknob, and passed the threshold. The TV glowed with that eerie purple light, spewing forth expressions of malevolence. I took one timorous step at a time, closing the distance between the front door and the television. Once there, I raised the hammer above my head and smashed the curved screen. Then I smashed it again. I trounced the machine. The machine from hell.

Bright red blood gushed from the cabinet of the television. Gallons, quarts, whatever. It spilled in quantity, inundating the carpet with clotting blood. Seizing my purse from the kitchen table, and my pistol from the silverware drawer, I ran from the sanguineous cataract.

I raced outside to my car. When I stepped off the porch, though, I found myself in water mid-calf deep. I sloshed to the car and climbed in. I turned the key, but the engine would not turn over. I raised my eyes — the hood was open, and the engine was drenched.

A Humvee with a searchlight approached along the road. The glowing windows of my house had attracted the attention of a search-and-rescue patrol. Soldiers rushed to my rescue and carried me to the federal building in town. I brought the familiar inquisitor up to date, and I passed last night on a sofa in a waiting room, wondering what the government was doing besides asking questions.

The usual driver in the blue uniform took me home in the morning. Although the rain and percussion of the thunder persisted, the house and environs looked quiet. The evil lights had faded, and the clerical banshee was gone. The helpful driver pushed my car into the garage for me, so it could dry out. I returned to the house and lay down upon my bed, utterly undone.

* * *

I awoke in darkness. Cats filled my room and a dozen were arranged in a circle around my bed, fixing their gazes upon me. I thought they must be hungry. Then, I heard the preacher's haranguing from the other side of my closed bedroom door. He continued the curdling refrain of death to humanity, of the removal of human refuse from the earth.

How? I had destroyed the television.

The door opened a crack, and purple light seeped through the space between the door and the frame. I sat halfway up, clutching my blanket — and feeling for my purse with the pistol. The door suddenly flew open revealing a gigantic midnight black cat — as big as me — who entered the room, standing upon its hind legs and walking upright. Both eyes sparkled like gemstones, and its fur was velvety and sleek.

A collar set with opals and rubies encircled its neck.

Raindrops pounded the bedroom window, while thunder reverberated in surround sound. With a great crack, glass sprayed in every direction, as a branch propelled by the wind shot right through the window and landed in the bedroom.

I lunged for the open window.

The monstrous cat reached it first.

"Who are you?" I implored. "What are you?"

"I am the prince of a distant sphere," he replied, purring in the voice of the televangelist of Armageddon. "My peaceable realm is suffering its death throes; we are the collateral damage of nuclear warfare amongst the human beings who inhabit the neighboring planets. The beasts who rained down from the firmament are my emissaries. They bravely navigated many universes in search of a new home for our kind. Notwithstanding the unfortunate discovery of my gallant scouts that people — a rodent species known throughout the universe for its insatiable appetite — plague this bounteous planet, we have chosen this globe for colonization. My swelling waters will cleanse the Earth of the human pestilence. We are aware that the human animals are gathering their forces, but all weapons of the cunning beasts cannot hold back my decontaminating flood."

"What do you wish of me?" I asked.

"You alone, Dear Lady, shall be spared, and your own domestic creatures, for your benevolence surpasses that of your species, and your singular devotion to felines is renowned. You shall be the Matriarch of a new type. The offspring of our own union, with the cosmic beasts who are evacuating even now from my dying realm, shall re-people this soon-to-be desolated planet. Lady Angelique, you shall be sainted above all mothers, honored above all cat fanciers, enthroned in Cat Heaven."

I had always been a cat lady, so accepting the cat's offer was not a terribly difficult decision.

"So be it," I said.

I requested, and was granted a boon, the companionship of my friends, who were spared also from the deluge and who would assist in the Cosmic Cat colonization of the Earth. I scratched the Prince's ears, and he licked my face. Then I gave him a good brushing, and a large saucer of milk.

* * *

This is the accurate and true history of our breed, and the illustrious pedigree of our race, who are descended from Lady Angelique and the Cosmic Cat, handed down from time immemorial through the ages, as told by Our Beloved Lady to the venerable Chronicle Cat in the Year of Our Cat Anno Felix I.

Katherine Kerestman is the author of multiple books, including Lethal, Haunted House and Other Strange Tales, and Creepy Cat's Macabre Travels: Prowling around Haunted Towers, Crumbling Castles, and Ghoulish Graveyards. She is a co-editor of The Weird Cat and Shunned Houses: An Anthology of Weird Stories, Unspeakable Poems, and Impious Essays. Katherine has additionally more than 60 short stories, poems, and essays in numerous online and print publications. Her education is in English and history, with a B.A. from John Carroll University and a M.A. from Case Western Reserve University. Katherine is a member of the Science Fiction and Fantasy Writers Association, the Jane Austen Society of North America, Mensa, the Horror Writers Association, the H.P. Lovecraft Historical Society, and the Dracula Society. She is also a raving Dark Shadows and Twin Peaks aficionado.

198

XII

The Silver Buckle

By: Angelique Fawns

The Silver Buckle

L una rubbed her eyes, her vision blurry from not getting her usual solid five hours of sleep. How could she sleep with those weird blinking lights in the sky? She spent the night with her nose pressed against the window. Even her meditation app couldn't lull Luna into dreamland.

Her parents had invited Luna to join them for a day in the city — but she had work to do. She wasn't like her folks; happy to live on inherited land for the rest of their lives. She had goals. Barrel racing. National Finals Rodeo goals. You had to be one of the best riders on Earth to win a big silver NFR buckle. At nineteen, she had to hustle before she grew too old.

Luna sipped coffee so hot it burned her tongue as she walked out to the barn. Her family farm had a cinematic view of Toronto. The cityscape was directly south with a sprawling view of skyscrapers and Lake Ontario. An hour from Toronto … and thousands of miles from her dreams. Canada was nice, but you had to go south of the border to Texas or Oklahoma to make it big in rodeo on a PRCA circuit. She adjusted her AirPods as a motivational podcast droned in her ears.

You are the one who can shape your existence. You possess the power to realize your dreams.

Luna had a silver buckle to win, and her horse wasn't going to train herself, was she? The wind picked up as the sky darkened. Her stomach clenched. She hated riding in the rain. Was that a thunderstorm rolling in over the lake?

A supersonic screech pierced her skull as a black, cylindrical thing dropped out of the sky. With the same eerie blinking lights from last night. Black evil spikes covered its visible surface, like a sea urchin descending from space — so enormous her mind froze. Worse than eating a carton of ice cream in only a couple of minutes. A flash shot out from the sea urchin's belly and Toronto exploded. Flames licked the air. Black smoke broiled. Explosions popped all over like corn kernels.

Luna gasped, her guts felt like they were filling with dry ice. Forget brain freeze, this was total body freeze.

Booms followed several seconds later. Her teeth chattered as the earth shook. This couldn't be happening. She turned up the audio on her podcast. The soothing male voice took her away from the moment.

You create your own reality. Your brain can create the world that you want. Envision it. Manifest it. Gratitude will create abundance. See the future that you want.

Luna didn't want to see a saucer in the sky. She turned north. Where the view turned into a peaceful field of green. Everyone knew aliens were just the fevered brainchildren of conspiracy theorists. She was seeing things.

This podcast, *Powerful Potential*, was changing her life. She needed to win a buckle and start building her barrel racing resume.

We all exist in a Quantum Quandary. The only limitations are in your mind.

Luna ignored the panic threatening to throw her into flight or fight. What did her therapist always say? Don't flip your lid. Stay rational.

ALIEN INVASION?

No. That wasn't rational.

Her brain refused to acknowledge it.

Say your dreams as if you are living them already.

She complied and started chanting, ignoring the Boombastic noise coming from the space urchin that wasn't in the sky.

"I am so grateful I am living a life where I can ride my horse every day while I passively make millions off my TikTok account," Luna called out, using her full lung capacity. "I'm so grateful I will be moving to Texas and hitting the rodeo circuit. I am a world-renowned barrel racer. That championship buckle is on my belt."

Luna's hand strayed to the top of her jeans. She wore a belt. But it sure didn't include any silver-winning buckle. She took a deep, shuddering breath. What was that smell? A cinnamon-meets-new-car odor. Chemical and bizarre. Alien fuel maybe? Her heart rate doubled. Sweat dripped down her back.

Luna shook her head violently. She wasn't living in lack or fear. She chided herself. Continue the mantra —

"I am visualizing rounding the third barrel, winning the go round at the finals. It's wonderful to live in a world where a what-the-hell-is-happening spaceship isn't blowing up Toronto."

Cerebral chaos fought for attention in her cortex. Her amygdala was taking over. Flipping her lid.

Fear. Fight. Flight. Panic.

Her eyes stung from sweat dripping down her face. Luna swallowed a hysterical giggle. She could create her own reality, right? One where her world was not being invaded by —

WHAT THE HELL WAS THAT SPIKY BLACK URCHIN SHIP IN THE SKY?

Luna slapped her cheek.

Don't look. Don't look.

Keep walking to the barn.

Despite what she told herself, Luna still turned and stared. South. The once-pristine skyline of skyscrapers had become a smoking haze.

No peak of the CN Tower. No bank buildings on Bay Street.

A low rumble shook the ground. She gasped, almost losing her balance.

She chased away insanity with another chant.

"Imagine that silver buckle. See 'PRCA Champion' etched on it. Manifest the buckle! I am grate —"

More low explosions and distant sirens interrupted her attempts to distract herself. Luna fell to her knees. The podcast still played in her ear pods.

Become what you envision. Fulfill your desires. It's all about successful habits.

Luna scrambled back to her feet.

"Keep thinking of that buckle!" she shouted. "Do not look at the city. Do not wonder why your parents aren't back yet."

She practiced every day in the pen her father had made for her. Three steel barrels in the dirt. Her father (Oh my God, Dad, are you dead? You must be dead!) religiously drove the tractor around to keep her practice area harrowed and level.

Being successful means having successful habits. Focusing fully on what you want to achieve.

Luna's thighs twitched as she imagined galloping a flawless cloverleaf pattern and hearing the roar of the rodeo crowd. This was her habit. Her number one priority in life. Weather, politics, whatever was going on in the city be damned.

Luna grew determined to win the RAM Rodeo buckle for barrel racing! Nothing was going to get in her way. Not an alien invasion. Not some black sea urchin of death. Not anything.

Her amygdala kicked in again. A black swirl of panic threatened to overwhelm her resolve. But Luna had meditative practice. Nothing could filch her focus.

Dreams only come true if you let nothing get in your way. Keep focused.

She couldn't help herself. Luna took another look at the huge black ship. Those spikes were so evil. Plumes of black smoke wafted high into the atmosphere. How long till it drifted here?

No. It wasn't happening. She walked into the barn. Windy was wild-eyed in her stall. Rushing back and forth. Bouncing off one wooden side to the other.

Luna raised her hand to the bars of the horse's stall.

"It's okay, Windy. Just don't look up when we get out there."

Another low boom shook the ground. Luna gasped and her horse reared, her pointy black ears grazing the roof's wooden beams.

"Easy girl," Luna cooed. "Let's go for a wee ride. Nothing disrupts our routine."

She grabbed her western saddle and threw it on Windy's back. The horse pranced but Luna managed to secure the cinch and slip a bridle on. She put on her helmet, led the horse out, and pulled herself up into the saddle.

Her head throbbed as another boom echoed over the farm. Windy scooted sideways, almost unseating Luna.

She grabbed a handful of black mane and managed to stay on.

"Whoa."

Windy snorted. Luna grimaced; the charred cinnamon smell had grown stronger. The sky turned an odd purple color. Etching the sky like northern lights, streaking and throbbing.

Windy broke into a froth and spun a few circles. Luna's sweaty hands almost lost their grip on the reins. They were both soaked with perspiration. A team of sweat hogs. Matching pit stains. Luna laughed hysterically.

Was she going mad?

Greatness comes from those who preserve and believe.

Luna dug her spurs into Windy's sides, and the mare leaped forward.

"Focus, focus, focus. It's fine, fine, fine."

She chanted with every step. They were making their way to the practice pen, but it was an ugly dance.

Luna peered through the gloom at her first barrel. Her stomach fluttered as Windy reared again, snorting and roaring. Her airway was already blocked. Windy only had one run in her today. She wouldn't even bother warming the horse up.

Another boom from the city. Another rear from Windy. This time, the horse stood straight up on her hind end and Luna almost tumbled off backward.

Almost.

She repositioned herself in the saddle when Windy came down on all four legs again.

"We are so grateful we are PRCA Rodeo Champions!"

Time to leave it all in the chute. Go for broke. Ride the race of her life.

Luna coughed. The air was thickening with the aftermath from whatever destroyed—

NO!

She wouldn't allow her thoughts to go there. Cowgirls don't cry. They ride. She clucked and kicked Windy's side.

The mare bounded forward, Luna feeling massive muscles contract and extend beneath her. She pointed Windy at the first barrel and loosened the reins. Her horse flew towards the barrel and rounded it expertly as Luna hung onto the horn.

Windy's breath filled Luna's ears. The roar. The roar was her horse, right? Not anything else –

Through the gloom, the second barrel beckoned.

Luna let go of the horn and put the reins up her neck to urge Windy faster. It was getting darker. Hard to see the exact spot to ask for the turn. Guessing, she dropped the outside rein, grabbed the horn, and Windy dropped her shoulder into the turn.

Another loud boom and the Good-Lord-I-don't-know-what-the-Hell-that-thing-is floated over them. The spiky ship. The black urchin of the end times.

You cannot stop. That is the first and last rule of success.

Luna felt a ripple run through her horse's muscles. Windy kept dropping and gave a ferocious buck. Luna managed to hold on for the first one, but then Windy followed up with two rapid kicks. The horse rounded her back like a bronc and lunged into the air. Luna's feet fell out of her stirrups and her body flew out of her saddle. She catapulted so quickly, she didn't even have time to prepare for the impact.

Smashing to the ground headfirst, her neck twisted at an unnatural angle as the rest of her body crumpled up behind Luna.

Wow, this must be what a car crash feels like.

Why doesn't my body hurt?

Luna heard, rather than saw, Windy gallop back for the barn. Her hooves beat a quick staccato. A drumbeat. A soundtrack to Luna's crash to the ground. Crash back to reality.

She wasn't a pro rodeo rider. She wasn't manifesting her success. At least not in this realm.

Where was she?

Alone in the dirt.

Staring up at the sky.

Only now did her brain allow her to see. To really see her current reality. The circular mass. The pulsing lights. Those black spikes. The ship now hovered directly over the farm.

An odd sensation filled her body as it lifted, arms dangling as she rose. A beautiful feeling. Her stomach relaxed. The headache fled.

Luna would become a human god to the aliens. She would manifest a life of galactic abundance. She could choose her reality. Luna would explore the universe, living a new existence of wonder.

The underside of the spaceship was covered in black protrusions.

But the door was silver. A square silver portal to her destiny. She took a deep breath and cinnamon filled her nostrils. Along with new car promise. What an amazing odor.

Luna soaked it all in.

As she passed through the opening, it struck her. The door was square and silver. Like a buckle. Just like a winning rodeo buckle.

She had manifested her dream.

Angelique Fawns is a journalist and speculative fiction writer. She began her career writing articles about naked cave dwellers in Tenerife, Canary Islands. After selling her first story to EQMM, she fell in love with weird fiction, which is ACTUALLY stranger than non-fiction. You can find her lurking at @angeliquefawns on X, Blogging about upcoming calls at https://angelique mfawns.substack.com, or gazing into the abyss hoping it stares back at her. More than 80 stories published. Find some in Mystery Tribune, Amazing Stories, and Space & Time.

XIII

Gamma Day

By: Phillip Carter

Gamma Day

Amber's thumbs traced cartoon blackberries on the side of the faded jar. She moved to unscrew the lid, hesitated, and put the jar back on the dusty shelf. A single ancient light bulb swung idly in the cold exhalations of the underworld, casting a yellow hue over everything.

"How long do we have to wait?" she asked.

"Until we nearly starve," Onyx said. Her sister had been named after an unusual jar in the larger storage halls, one containing an old plastic toy. The toy, Onyx, was a Roborider, a hybrid of motorcycle and robot, not unlike the machines now idly roaming the scorched earth above, their hive mind fried by Gamma Day. Amber smiled weakly at her sister, remembering seeing her sweep the surface, riding one of the braindead Searchers like a motorcycle.

"Talk about nominative determinism," she mumbled now, echoing what she said at the time, watching her sister unload an electron rifle toward one of the invaders.

"What?" Onyx asked, snapping Amber back into the present.

"Nothing. Just miss the surface. You never taught me how to ride the Searchers."

"In my defense, it started raining acid."

"There's always an excuse," Amber joked.

"Always."

They left the pantry, exited through an old maintenance door, and hopped down onto the train tracks. Onyx placed their loot gently in the cart. Handprints of biolights shone bluely against the subway walls, replacing long-ago crumbled posters. Pools and ponds of biolights had condensed in between tracks and in ancient toilets and bathroom sinks, each bringing with them the flora and fauna of the new world. The space moss was a favourite for Amber, an ochre-yellow lichen that had become ubiquitous in the living underworld, its alien spores carried on those rhythmic exhalations that provided clean air to the humans and their pets.

All things considered; the end of the world wasn't that bad.

Onyx climbed up onto the opposite platform, and together they braved a loftier portion of the underground. They activated their torches and scaled the ancient tubes of the place, unlocked what was once a ticket booth, now a fortified defense structure, and passed through to the unmanaged world. Onyx hit the button operating the lights in this section.

"How close are we?" Amber asked.

"To the surface?"

"Yeah."

"A few stairways."

"Can they hear us?"

"If they're at the entrances, definitely."

"We should go back."

"It was your idea, Amber," Onyx said.

She had left her torch on, just in case the lights failed.

"I won't be long."

Amber walked away, looking at the ruins of an old convenience store between the lower levels and the surface.

"What are you doing?"

"I've ran out of books to read," Amber lied.

Her sister illuminated her way with the torch despite the lights, electron rifle by her side. The back of the little store was just dark enough for something small and slim to hide in there. Some surviving invaders could fit there in the shadows, waiting to pounce.

"Anyone in there?" Onyx asked.

"Shopkeeper."

"Dead?"

"I should hope so, his head is missing," Amber announced.

She knelt behind a bookshelf, causing Onyx no small anxiety, and started rustling around with her own torch, knocking over ancient books with her pistol, pawing her way around the shelves.

"Anything I might like?" Onyx asked.

"Cookery book."

"All the world's food is spoiled."

Amber laughed.

"A climate change magazine."

"Too late for that."

"Self-help," Amber said, sliding one of twenty copies out across the floor. Onyx looked down at it, at the smiling pre -apocalyptic woman on the pale green cover.

"Too late for that too," she said, glancing up again. "Any fiction?"

"Escapism?"

"Yeah. Can't get enough."

Amber emerged from behind the shelves.

"There's this Rod Grasper story."

"Trash."

"What about this?"

Amber held up a happy looking book about a sailing trip.

"Do you think the reefs are still out there somewhere?" Onyx asked.

"I thought you wanted escapism."

"I do. I want something unreal, not something that reminds me the world ended."

"Then there's nothing really here," Amber said. "All boring, normal people books

She looked over the shelf, waited for Onyx to briefly check the surroundings, and secreted a small brown book inside her coat. She got up, walked back out of the little store, stopped, and looked up the stairs.

"Sense anything?" Onyx asked.

"No. I just miss the sun."

"It'll still be there when we next go out."

"You can't promise that. They could have taken it."

"Then the planet would freeze, and the ice would crawl down these tunnels and suffocate us as we sleep," Onyx said. "We would know."

"Cheerful."

The pair made their way back into the underground, locked the gates, and passed through the tunnels without incident. The world's new quietness was no match for the hideous noise inside their heads, the thumping of their hearts when a cat knocked over something on the higher levels, when the natural ebb and flow of the world's heat caused ancient tracks to creak, or tunnels to wheeze as if the mouth of some giant beast. This world once wanted them dead, and now it was dead itself, passing forth through that fungal stage before a total rebirth.

"What will the new world be like?" Amber asked.

She stroked the space moss as they made their way downstairs. Thicker patches would retract like anemones.

"I think it will be quiet," Onyx said. "But I worry that moss has a central hive mind somewhere, that when we climb up out of our caves, it will claim the surface is its own and push us back down here."

"It's just moss," Amber said.

"And the biolights are just biolights, but that doesn't mean there aren't people trying to figure out how to talk to them."

"Yeah," Amber passed a glowing blue handprint on the wall, and wondered who had put it there.

"A whole world fell on our heads. Then the invaders came. Then Gamma Day. Something up there fried them, fried a few of us too."

"Could have been a cosmic event," Amber suggested.

Onyx remembered the small throne of science books her younger sister had amassed. She had noticed the girl picking up another book from the bookshop but chose to feign ignorance.

"You doing any research lately?"

"That's why we were at the bookshop," Amber said, semi honestly.

They got back down to the station.

Amber balanced herself on the track, placing one foot tentatively ahead of the next. If she had been born earlier, or somewhere with more books, she might have compared herself to an acrobat, that word which now was slipping away into the past. Onyx smiled as she looked back at her, seeing in her playfulness the child she had rescued from the surface colonies and brought down to safety in the tubes. Every time she thought about it, she remembered the heat of the alien's laser rifles firing overhead as she pushed the child down into the city's drains.

"What is it?" Amber asked.

"Remembering the day we met," Onyx admitted.

"Happy memory?"

"Just glad you're still here. That we became sisters."

Onyx climbed into the cart. Amber clambered in behind her, checked both their heads were against the pillows, and pressed the accelerator. The beheaded Searcher revved its bastardised engine and started spinning its wheels. They whirred loosely against the track, then slotted into place, launching the minecart forward with a jolt.

"Fucking hell!" Onyx yelped.

"Need a new pillow?" Amber said.

"Need a new spine."

"We'll scour the body fields when its dry and dark," Amber joked.

The memory of that place opened a new track for the carriage of their conversation.

"Don't *derail* this nice day out," Onyx joked.

"Day 'out'?"

"Good point." Onyx watched the tunnels ahead. "Gallery detour?"

"Sure," Amber said.

She turned back, looking at the open neck of the Searcher bot, her eyes following the wires trailing from its neural stump to the buttons welded to the back of the minecart. Amber pressed a button, and the signal ahead changed, letting other Searcher carts know of their location, direction, speed, and intent. Rails snapped into place, and within a few minutes they had slowed, waited for a supply vessel to pass, and smiled as the driver tipped his hat. The Searcher welded to their cart accelerated again, pressing the minecart toward the gallery.

Humans, now like ants whose nests they had once usurped to create highways and canals and trainlines, had become a subterranean species themselves, without much fanfare. Perhaps the psychological embers of the Second World War were still aglow in the British spirit, because by the time the Third World War fell from the sky, they had no issue with filing themselves away into subways, coal mines, and missile silos across the country. Now, the world's new cavemen and cavewomen had burrowed their way between some of these disparate colonies, surviving in a new world that honoured the old through its strange new religions and traditions.

Soon enough, they reached the gallery. This stretch of subway was decorated with the combined treasures the humans had managed to salvage from the surface, known colloquially as upstairs. Everything from foil birthday balloons to priceless paintings were collected here, connected together with red string. The whole museum was a process, a method of discovery. Every time a scavenger returned alive from upstairs, they added something to this museum, and the curators made a desperate, but informed attempt at placing it in this tremendous timeline.

Amber leaned out of the minecart as it slowed, passing the astronomy section. A huge plastic moon rested on the station platform, now a display case. It had been rolled in from the surface to an underground tunnel some years ago and, for several hours, blocked one of the main ventricles of the heart of the new world. It was bracketed on either side by mannequins dressed as David Bowie and Freddie Mercury, both of which were damaged and partially melted, though some attempts had been made to restore them.

"Saint Mercury and Bowie were scarecrows once, before the rain turned murderous," Onyx said.

She tapped the lightning bolt on her purple leather jacket, lifted an index finger to her upper lip, showcasing a tattoo of a bushy moustache.

"And their music spoke to the stars, I remember," Amber said.

"Are you disinterested?"

"No. Just showing you I remember."

"Good. Well, you did want the tour," Onyx said.

They trundled alongside the Bowie and Mercury mannequins, both entranced by the acid damage done to them.

"Who's your favourite?" Amber asked.

She grinned deviously as Onyx turned back frowning, still not able to parse the question.

"To pick a favourite would be to call the other a non-favourite, and I can't do that to Freddie," she said.

"Last month you said you couldn't do it to Bowie," Amber said.

"I could definitely do it to Bowie."

"Gross."

"Anyway," Onyx said, passing a heavy jar of something back to Amber, "Mercs and Bow-Bow were the humble defenders of our wheat yield before God started pissing lava on our dreams. When I swiped them up the first storm had already got to them, but I think they're doing pretty well considering."

"I heard it can eat through concrete," Amber said.

"I'm doubtful. The tunnels are so old now, without proper maintenance. I think the fact none of us go outside any more is probably why they're crumbling. Cities aren't like bodies, Amber, when they decay there's no medicine for them, no healing. You just have to swap out the old parts for new ones."

"Or design structures that can feed and fix themselves."

"Like the invader towers?"

"Exactly."

"You're full of good ideas," Onyx said. "If the universities were still up there, you'd beat all of them."

"I don't think you could 'beat' a university," Amber said, taking the wooden lid off the heavy wide jar Onyx had given her.

They passed now into the sea life section. Amber did not look into the heavy jar, not yet. Her favourite part of the gallery was coming up.

"You know what I mean," Onyx said.

"I do."

Above and ahead of them, a whale's skeleton had been positioned in the subway so the cart would pass through its glittering, decorated bones. The whale's head loomed ahead of them, a false jaw extending from its real jaw so the minecart could move 'through' without damaging the skeleton. The lights in this section were dimmed and filtered through deep blue glass, vases and tiles and broken windows taped up and glued into place. Ribbons of blue-green plastic sheeting flapped in the rhythmic inhales and exhales of the lungs of the underworld, and the combined effect was a simulation of underwater life. For now, Amber didn't look into the jar. As usual, she was bewitched by the alien magic of this underwater world.

"Listen," she said gently.

"To what?" her sister asked.

"When the minecart trundles over the tracks and we go under the ribs, it feels like the noise is from the ribs, like we're a krill being eaten," Amber said, eyes wide with wonder.

"I love you Amber," Onyx said.

"Why?"

"You're like the old world. So full of wonder even down here."

"I still remember it, a little," Amber said, her voice even softer now.

They passed under the whale's ribcage, through to the tail, and to the edge of this station platform. The cart came to a stop. Amber looked back at the Searcher and its neural stump, burnt and decayed. She remembered them tearing through the buildings, huge and indefatigable.

"When I was small, they were massive," she said.

"I know. Do you want to explore a bit?"

"Yeah."

The two sisters crawled out of the minecart, and the Searcher bot shunted itself out of the way of any incoming traffic, lobbing the metal cart onto the unused track to the right. It wasn't a perfect system, but with minimal traffic, and most people only going one way on the now-cleared circular lines, it made the most sense.

Amber climbed onto the tiled platform and looked toward Freddie Mercury and the moon. From here she could not see David Bowie, but she could make out the tips of his dancing shoes. She moved to an old metal bench in the subway, which had been overtaken with space moss and then cleaned again, leaving a polished chrome where the moss had grown and eaten the rust. Amber sat down carefully and finally lifted the wooden lid off the large, wide jar.

"A candle?"

"A scented candle," Onyx smiled.

"Why's it so heavy?"

"Just say thank you and sniff the bloody thing."

Amber sniffed shallowly, tentatively, then changed her mind. She took in the entire smell of the thing. It overpowered the grassy, dusty smell of these fringes of the subway system, and for a moment the cool air breathing in and out of the underworld aligned with her inhalation. She closed her eyes and remembered her childhood, before the invaders landed and the world turned against itself. She remembered a world before Searchers, where motorcycles were not threats, but interesting, rare vehicles she saw zooming down the street outside her house every summer. They were not gunmetal and teal and slim like the Searchers, but big and colourful, ridden by men and women in leather jackets not unlike Onyx's.

Yes, it was all coming back now.

"The memories are washing in, like waves on the shore," she told her older sister.

Onyx said nothing, stood there smiling, but forever vigilant. She checked the tunnels out of habit and, in this brief moment, Amber remembered they were both armed, that death still lurked around a corner somewhere, that it was a gamble finding out which corner it waited around.

"Your tribe did well, surviving all that time above ground."

"The sky bombs helped, by the time the aliens got to us they were dying, demented."

"Still dangerous though," Onyx said.

"Yeah. And they left their poisons behind."

Onyx nodded somberly, remembering the corpses the toddler ambled between.

"Alien neurotoxin didn't affect children as bad," she said.

"No."

"Some stunted development, not much else."

"Yeah," Amber said.

She sniffed the candle again.

"You're smart now, imagine how smart you'd be without brain poison."

"I'm washing it out with this candle," Amber joked.

"Chocolate," she added, eyes wide. She pawed the jar for a label, but it had long ago perished.

"I think cocoa and orange, maybe some sandalwood," Onyx said, looking at her sister in her peripheral vision, her mind and eyes elsewhere.

The undead Searcher twitched.

"A vehicle yearns for its rider," she said, memorising an old phrase her trainer taught her.

"What?"

"Catbike's noticed something," she said darkly.

"I hate that word," Amber said. "They're nothing like cats."

She glanced at her older sister, and immediately Onyx recognised that childlike panic.

"You're right," she said. "Cats are slimmer, more agile. But it was a long time ago, before we started being clever with words again. And my bike did look like a cat. I painted whiskers on it. I miss it. Now come on, we've got to go."

"What is it?" Amber asked.

She stood up from the metal bench. The station lights flickered off for a split second, and biolight puddles appeared for that instant like constellations in the night sky. Somehow, both sisters knew what the other was thinking; it had been far too long since they visited the surface, and perhaps now was the right time.

"Upstairs?" Onyx asked nervously.

"What have you seen?" Amber asked.

"Nothing. It's a feeling," Onyx admitted.

She imagined her sister would not be interested in feelings, but the younger woman sealed the candle and took Onyx by the hand, saying nothing at all. The pair glanced briefly at the tunnel they had come from, two sets of eyes hunting for something waiting in the darkness. Onyx took the rifle from her back, aimed its rectangular nozzle down the tunnel, and considered firing a warning shot. The undead Searcher clunked itself back onto the main line.

"There could be someone down there, or someone's pet."

"Yeah," Onyx said.

All at once Amber remembered the night the spires fell. The invasion came and went in a matter of days, but the apocalyptic aftermath spread like a cancer through the surviving world.

"The nukes spilled that alien biosphere over the world, and we still haven't seen everything that fell from the guts of that ship," Onyx said. "How do I know there's not something worse down here, in older tunnels, chasing us, hunting us, even now?"

"The gamma ray burst fried the world," Amber tried to reassure her. "We kept the invaders out, and they died out there."

"How do we know the space moss, or the biolights, aren't talking to them?"

The pair waited as the Searcher clicked and whirred, spinning its wheel idly against the greasy old tracks.

"Come on you stupid fuck!" Onyx yelped.

She leaned over and hit the robot.

"Like that will do anything," Amber said, aiming her pistol down the other tunnel.

A few excruciating seconds passed, and finally the machine clicked onto the grooves and powered forward. Onyx was slammed against the side of the cart, and in her panic fired off a shot which dissolved Freddie Mercury's arm. Once the green light of the blast faded, four reptilian eyes stared out from the dark tunnel, coupled with the soft glow of an orange visor above it.

"Shit!" she said.

"What?" Amber asked, not looking back.

"Melted Merc's fucking arm."

"Is that it?"

Onyx didn't reply.

"I said is that it?" Amber asked again.

She trained her gun on the tunnel ahead. The Searcher spoke in its invisible signals to others in the network, reporting the gunfire as an obstruction in the road. By now other Searcher carts in the network would be chirping their dire warnings to other survivors in the underworld. Something was happening on the gallery wing.

The beast lumbered out of the darkness, hurtling through the gallery station at the same rate as the accelerating minecart.

"Onyx," Amber's teeth clattered nervously. "What is it?"

"Just shut up, I'm aiming."

The beast got closer, four eyes rolling in its mad head and rotten forelimbs replaced by robotic prosthetics. The rider carried a rifle of their own, not too dissimilar to Onyx's. It was one of the dregs of the invader army, a survivor that had somehow managed to keep itself hidden all this time.

Onyx squeezed the trigger, and a bolt of energy shot past the beast's head, obliterating a portion of the subway wall. The creature continued its pursuit unfazed. Amber didn't have to ask if Onyx hit her target. She still heard the beast's relentless galloping behind the Searcher bot's whirring wheels.

"DOWN!!!" Onyx shouted.

The noise alone scared Amber into the cart before her brain fully registered the word. A beam of greenish light screamed through the air like a banshee, singing Onyx's black hair and grazing her jacket sleeve as she aimed her rifle. She slumped back for a second, played it down, got back in position.

Onyx squeezed the trigger again, ever so slightly, so that one jolt, one twitch would send the energy bolt down the tunnel. She had memorised the network, and she knew a curve lay ahead, a superelevation that the beast would not expect. She knew it was looking at the gun, and she knew it expected her to shoot straight for it. But there would be a moment, a split second where she could get away with firing off to one side, and the beast, not wanting to smash its slathering head into a wall, would run straight into the bolt.

She fixed the rifle on the back of the cart.

The invader fired again, this time missing completely.

The minecart turned, and Onyx pulled the trigger.

The creature's head exploded in a cloud of glittering green light.

The rider fell off, leaving one of their arms behind in the tunnel.

She fired another energy pulse down the winding track, clipping the alien rider, shaving off the front of their chest. As the light faded, she saw their organs spilling out.

"It's done," she sighed, finally allowing herself to breathe.

"What the fuck was it?" Amber asked, her pistol still trained ahead.

"Some new thing. Ugly fucker," Onyx replied.

She looked down inside the minecart, checked the jars they had brought from the pantry.

"Had a rider, one sec. Fuck. We lost a jam in the chaos," she said sadly.

"Which one?"

"Cherry I think."

"Can you scoop it back in?"

"No, can't really discern between jam and arm blood right now."

"What?"

Amber turned around.

"Turn back. I'll sort it. Need you scouting."

The minecart trundled along, but the Searcher bike welded to its back had been wounded in the battle also. The vehicle moved sluggishly, stumbling with its damaged wheel against the harder turns and struggling through puddles of biolight.

"Sorry I didn't wrap your present," Onyx said.

"No use wasting paper," Amber replied, her eyes fixed on the tracks ahead.

A minute of dark silence followed, during which both sisters considered a world in which the other had not survived. Amber reached down into the cart with her free hand, passing her sister a small book.

"What's this?" Onyx asked.

"Old dictionary. Pre-war words, pre-world words. I think these were old before the war."

"It's for me?"

"I know you like songs. Thought you'd figure out Bowie's lyrics with it."

"He was a cryptic bugger," Onyx admitted. "Thanks."

"How's the arm?"

"It's skin deep, a long cut. Looks worse in the dark, feels worse."

"You sure?"

"If I was lying, I'd have bled out by now," Onyx said.

"No you wouldn't, you'd have eventually, reluctantly, asked for help."

"True."

The infirmary wasn't far from the gallery, locked behind several improvised doors that had been reinforced over the years. The first few were made from the roofs of several cars, welded together with electron rifles in the hasty early days of the invasion. Beyond this were doors crafted from old oak bookshelves, then an industrial refrigerator. Beyond this was a short walk through a carved-out tunnel, then the secure space of a hollowed-out bank vault, its useless money used now as napkins, bandages, notepads, and scrunched up toys for the infirmary's countless cats. The vault door was never opened, as rubble buried it on the other side. It stood now as a symbol of the relative security of this little, strange place.

Onyx lay in a bed between two piles of worthless money, her rifle close to her side. A doctor tried to move it, to better reach her arm, but she refused, pulling it closer.

"They won't wait for me to walk to the armoury and power up," she said.

The doctor nodded. He applied the medicine; some paste made from the ochre-yellow space moss. This was medicine, bandage, painkiller and suture. The moss offered everything humanity needed. The doctor crushed some more lichen into the mortar, crushing it with the pestle.

"No pills?" Onyx asked.

"We've cultivated a pill moss. Does the same thing, eats black mould."

"And I guess Amber helped you with the research?"

"Her pet mosses have been a great help," the doctor said.

Onyx hummed affirmatively. She inched up the bed, flicking through her new book. Amber sat beside her, legs crossed, and sniffed the candle again.

"Do you want a go on it?"

"Yes please."

Amber lifted the candle to Onyx's nose.

"Smells like those chocolates we lifted from that stockroom we found."

"Yeah."

The doctor applied another layer of paste, wrapped the wound in leaves, smiled and walked away.

"Oh, no itching it," he said.

"Can do, Doc."

"How are you feeling?" Amber asked.

Her older sister flicked through the book.

"Bit pissed off about my jacket."

"We're alive."

"I know, but the jacket was really nice."

"It still is really nice," Amber said.

"It's ruined."

"We can get another."

"Sure, we'll just phone the designer. Do we have a Ouija board here?"

"Fair point. But seriously. How are you really feeling?" Amber asked.

Onyx looked at her little sister, then around the infirmary. A pink plastic chandelier hung from one corner of the vault's ceiling, from which were suspended bags of medication, fluids, and blood transfusions. A poster of the David Bowie, Freddie Mercury, and the moon was pasted to one wall, taken on the day the gallery's current incarnation was finished. In several parts of this well-lit space, the individual vaults were used to house experiments with the space moss that had fallen down to earth. An aroma of fried doughnuts wafted in from another part of this base. Onyx thought about the demented movement of the invader and its broken, feral steed. An assistant showed up with sliced toast and jam.

"Good find," they said. "Smells nice."

"Take a slice," Onyx said.

The assistant gave the pair all but one half of a slice of toast and left. Onyx rested her toast on her lap; behind the book she could not yet put down.

"How am I feeling?" Oynx said, pondering Amber's earlier question aloud. "A simple question, but so many words."

"Would you be able to compress it down to one?" Amber asked.

Her sister raised a finger, winced in pain from the movement, and considered the words on the page in front of her.

"Thanks for this," Onyx said, waving the book.

"It's okay."

"I don't think I can compress it. It's big. I suppose I am feeling tired. The weight of all this time has caught up to me. When that creature shot at us, I remembered how I felt pushing you into those drains, away from your people, just to keep you alive."

"You did the right thing, they were stubborn. They wanted to keep me on the surface," Amber said. "And then Gamma Day came, killed most of the aliens, and most of my people."

"That's what's so heavy on my mind," Onyx said. "That it might happen again as soon as we resurface."

"But we can't not resurface. You wanted to see if the reefs were still there."

"True," Onyx said. "But it's such a grim celebration."

The two sisters finished their toast, taking turns reading the old book and sniffing the old candle. Onyx practically deflated in her hospital bed, finally releasing the pressure and stress that had been building up in her muscles since the day she adopted Amber as her sister.

"You're a little genius, you know," she said.

"So I've been told," Amber replied.

"That moss farm you've got going in your room, did that really become medicinal?"

"I think it was already evolving that way. I just selected for the patches which were the best at adapting to difficult environments, again and again, pushing evolution toward a space moss which can eat the black mould that's been ruining some of the subways."

"Just that?" Onyx asked sarcastically.

"Yeah."

"So nothing too big, just altering the evolution of an alien lifeform so that it helps us survive the aftermath of the day it crashed into Earth."

"Yeah. But to be fair, there's not much else to do down here," Amber joked.

"You're right. We should go outside."

Amber grinned and held her sister's hand.

"Really?"

"As soon as I'm out of the infirmary," Onyx said.

A day or so later, the pair were escorted by two others to the higher stairwells above the old midway point where the convenience store and barricades were. They stood now at the top of those wide stairwells and had only one more short stairway to ascend before they stood directly in the sunlight trickling down through the vines and shattered windows of the new world.

"Looks like they didn't eat the sun," Amber said.

"No."

The other two stayed behind Amber and Onyx, being too afraid of another Gamma Day to stand on the surface. Onyx climbed the final stairs and stepped out first, looking quickly and longingly at the sky, searching for alien ships, falling planetoids, acid rain clouds.

"It's a clear day," Amber said. "I remember these."

Her older sister took another step onto the abandoned street. Blackened scars of electron rifle fire marked the outside of the station, but most had been filled now with a darker, richer moss.

"New space moss!" Amber said.

"It matches your name," Onyx joked.

Amber knelt down in the street, saying 'hello' to a patch of moss, stroking it, scooping a loose piece up along with the rock it was growing on.

"Look at that," she said.

The moss had small tendrils which moved like the stuff in the subways, but with a rhythmic, almost deliberate pulse. Some of the tendrils opened into flowers, blue, yellow, pink.

"Hello," she said to the moss.

Blue — Yellow, flicked the moss's flowers.

"How are you?"

Blue — Pink — Yellow, flicked the flowers.

"Well, that's new," Amber said.

The moment was cut short. Onyx was already aiming her rifle down the street, the nozzle bristling with anxious energy.

"What is it?"

"Horses."

Down the street, behind an upturned bus, was a small herd of wild horses. They stared at Onyx and Amber with a mixture of surprise, and an almost genetic wisdom.

"Do you think they remember humans?" Onyx asked.

"Why?"

"Much better than some alien Searcher catbike."

A while later, once the horses had been tamed and ridden, the pair each rode a steed and felt the new Earth air rushing through their hair on empty streets, now turned to meadows. Amber and Onyx stopped by a rusting bridge above a dried river, now a valley jungle in the heart of London. Onyx had brought her Gamma Day gift, the brown book of forever-old words, to the surface with her.

"You asked me a few days ago how I was feeling," Onyx said. "Wanted me to compress it into one word."

"I did."

Amber watched parakeets flying through the crumpled remnants of an invader starship.

"Ask me again," Onyx said.

"Ask what?"

"How I am feeling," the older sister said.

"How are you feeling?" Amber asked.

Onyx touched a word in the old book, turning it so her sister, sitting beside her, could read the definition.

"Gruntled."

Phillip Carter is an award-winning comedian, award-winning poet, and not award-winning science fiction author because he'd rather spend his entry fee on Lego spaceships. He has told jokes about time travel to historians, and is currently trying to find a venue full of aliens for his probing material. His work brings together dark, existential themes with characters whose humour and resilience make them completely human. Apart from Lax Morales. He's a crab. You can find his books, jokes, and other things at linktr.ee/phillipcarter

XIV

Ascentia's Downfall

By: Winston Malone

Ascentia's Downfall

The commander's cabin was too large for one man, and not because it had a view of the Triangulum Galaxy. Orson Clark, lying on his oversized mattress in the stark chamber, watched the starlight float past on an unseen current, reminding him of home. He longed to return there, to rid himself of the responsibility thrust upon him. Corporate viewed him as a symbol, a leader. Clark was simply a survivor. And that's what mattered to him in the vast hostility of space.

Clark moved to his side to alleviate pain crawling up his spine. It retreated, then crept back in like a slow-rolling tide. The pain never left, not entirely. Most doctors said it never would. Drugs were an option, of course, but he refused them. Plus, the nightmares held him hostage, not the pain.

A holo clock on the wall showed several hours had passed, his sleep shift nearly halfway over. Clark was lucky to get two hours of rest, maybe three if the work shift had been especially grueling.

"ALI," he whispered.

"Yes, Commander?" The virtual assistant reciprocated his hushed tone. "What can I do for you?"

"Play the sounds of the ocean."

"Very well, Commander."

A soft hiss rose from hidden speakers like white noise. Then, a familiar crescendo landed with a crash. Gulls cawed in their distant, chaotic song. The tropical orchestra swept Clark's thoughts back to his childhood on Provo — the coastal cottage, his parents cooking dinner, and Derek, his older brother, calling out to play catch.

Clark felt sand nestled between his toes as his mind drank in the memory. A brine scent wafted along the ocean breeze. Heat radiated across his shirtless back and sweat glistened on his forearms. A pelican dove into the ocean and emerged with a catch sliding down its gullet. To him, this was paradise — nothing like it in all the known universe.

Derek threw the augment ball, a digital orb of light rendered by the lenses on their pupils. Clark laughed as he ran after the ball, which imitated the physics of a real one bouncing atop the sand. When he picked it up, his mind tricked him into feeling the augment's resistance as if he were there — still on the beach.

Wasn't he?

Clark turned to find a man in dark rags had replaced his brother. He swayed back and forth on the beach like a drunkard. The stranger lifted his hood, revealing an unkempt beard and tawny, rotted teeth. Black tears oozed down his cheeks and he pointed at Clark's hand. He no longer held an augment ball. Instead, the silver-cased device pulsed red, emanating rapid beeps. Clark drew his arm back to throw the grenade, but everything went white.

Clark woke, drenched in sweat, to an unscheduled alert from the cruiser's bridge. The nightmares always felt so real. His holo clock confirmed another hour had passed.

He threw back the blankets and sat up. The cabin's floor glowed brighter as ALI recognized his movements. Clark felt around for the wire attached to his spinal port. The implant needed routine charging to maintain full mobility. He unplugged the cable, and a tingling sensation remained around the port. The wire retracted into a small, black cylinder on the nightstand.

"ALI, connect me to the bridge."

A soft tone sounded.

"Commander Clark, sorry to wake you, but it appears we have a major problem," Sandy said.

Sandy Orion was Ascentia's navigator. Although ALI could control the massive cruiser independently, company regulation called for organic oversight to monitor space flight and assess further anomalies.

"What is it, Sandy? Aren't we still a couple hours from the Kal system?"

"Not exactly, Commander. It's hard to explain. You'll need to see it for yourself."

Clark thought he detected a hint of worry in her voice, which was unlike her. Sandy had been promoted to Class A navigator after years of intra-planetary shipping missions. She'd seen it all, and Clark had hand-picked her because he wanted someone with experience.

"On my way," he said

Clark got dressed. He zipped up his grey coat and glanced at the holo mirror. Grabbing the bottom of the coat with both hands, he tugged it down and straightened his back. He imagined hearing the whirr of tiny gears in the implant moving to his neural commands. But he knew that the technology was too advanced to emit any sound at all.

Grabbing the black cylinder from the nightstand, it automatically extended into a cane. A sliver of a Bal Aldorox crystal powering the cylinder shone a bright blue in the crest atop the cane. The device reminded him of his survival and his newfound purpose as a commander.

Walking with a limp, Clark made his way through bustling corridors to Acentia's bridge. It occupied the centermost compartment of the massive cruiser, cushioned by sections of the ship that, if damaged, sealed automatically to protect leadership and the navigation crew from the vacuum of space. Inside the large chamber, reinforced walls doubled as screens displaying the cruiser's surroundings via multispectral cameras, or MSCs, on the outer hull.

It felt like stepping directly into space.

"Finally, Commander. I mean…" Sandy paused, eyeing his cane. "Sorry, I didn't mean, um, you won't believe this."

She stepped out from the circle of consoles at the center of the room. Other crew members typed away at their stations.

"What do you see?" she asked.

Clark examined the screens and made a half-hearted attempt to absorb the live footage of space.

"I don't know, Sandy. Where am I looking?"

"Straight ahead." She pointed to what was essentially the nose of the cruiser. "Let me rephrase. What don't you see?"

Clark wasn't a navigator or a spectro-reader. To him, all he saw were dark, star-riddled images surrounding them on all sides.

"I see … nothing."

"Exactly."

"Wait. We are heading to the Kal system, right?"

"Yes, Commander, we are. That's the weird part. The MSCs aren't picking up new light from the direction of the Kal system's sun."

Sandy used her hands to select the area of space, and ALI, responding to her hand signals, zoomed the front screen to the desired location. The image on the wall lurched forward. Stars appearing on the screen didn't resemble average stars. They were deep red, like fresh blood spatter on a black canvas.

"I thought you said we weren't picking up light?" Clark said. "Aren't those red giants? What's so interesting about dying stars?"

"We're not picking up *new* light, sir," Sandy said. "These stars are supposed to be nearest to Ascentia, but based on the spectral readings, they're moving *away* from us."

Pain swelled in Clark's lower back. He shifted his weight to the cane. What Sandy said was impossible. Light didn't just decide to turn around and run from you when you approached it. Something interfered with its trajectory.

"A distortion field," he said.

"Yes, or something similar," Sandy replied. "It's not natural, to say the least. The perpetrator, for lack of a better term, must not want us to see what's happening in the Kal system. The spectro-readers and I believe it's a new type of technology."

Perpetrator. Clark didn't like the sound of that.

"I'm assuming we've calculated the shape of this supposed distortion field?"

"We'd need to run a virtual survey to map the precise dimensions, sir. But the current spectral readings suggest it's emanating from the planet of Kal Dera spherically, extending outward for several BAMs to encompass the entire system."

Bal Aldorax Minutes had become corporate's standard unit for measuring space travel since updating its fleet to run off the rare energy crystals. A ship equipped with a single crystal could reach a destination 16% faster than an object traveling at the speed of light. Ships powered by multiple Bal Aldorax crystals could travel at even quicker rates, their top speed determined by the size of the crystals and the type of spacecraft.

"We don't have the luxury of waiting for the board to convene and debate this strange development, not while in hostile territory." Scav ambushes on transient vessels had increased. Clark vowed he wouldn't make that mistake again. "Sandy, alert the AVR drivers. We need to know what we're dealing with before making any rash decisions."

He stepped past her to get a better look at the anomaly. Light moving backward? Exo-Humans had learned little about the Kal system, but it had been discovered as a viable Goldilocks planet. Could it be a local phenomenon, or had someone intentionally intercepted them?

Sandy turned to a young man sitting at one of the screens.

"Rob, let the augment team know they're conducting an official mission. Have any other users log out now."

The fresh-faced officer looked shocked at being addressed with the commander present. He sat up straight and cleared his throat, typing like a madman on his console.

"They've been notified, ma'am … and sir."

I knew it was too good to be true, Clark thought.

Corporate had sold him on Kal Dera being a tranquil retreat at the edge of civilization. But only one place qualified as paradise, and he silently prayed he'd stand on its peaceful shores again.

* * *

The Exo-Humans had long discovered that knowledge of the known universe changed at the speed of light. A visual distortion in space forcing light to move backward? Markos Talesko pondered the possibilities and concluded it was deliberate. And if they hadn't created it, who did? Scav or something worse?

Markos, Ascentia's chief augmenter, got to work in the Augmented Virtual Reality bay. He woke the entertainment chassis, or ECs, from their dormant state. Each chassis needed at least ten minutes to thoroughly scan the spatial environment surrounding Ascentia, including the planet they apparently orbited but could not see. The last chassis of eight booted up when a soft hand touched his shoulder.

"Hey, Honey."

Markos turned and looked up at his wife. He wrapped his arms around Laren and kissed her, pulling her closer so her belly pressed against his own. When he released her, Markos leaned down to touch her belly and speak to his daughter.

"Hey, little scout. Mom doesn't know it yet, but you'll be a fighter like me."

He peeked to see if Laren was scowling. She wasn't.

"Whoa, whoa, whoa."

A booming voice reverberated through the AVR bay from behind the couple. It belonged to Gareth, a stout, bearded man who was one of the other drivers.

"What's with all the lovey-dovey stuff?" he said. "I can't work in these conditions. Please make it stop."

"You work?" Markos said.

Gareth chuckled.

"Shut it. Ascentia wouldn't run a day without me here to fix up after y'all."

Markos regarded the six drivers trickling in after Gareth. He mock saluted, and they each returned the gesture. Vayto crudely modified his fingers while doing so, sparking a grin from Markos. On Ascentia, they were one giant family, which came with the good and the bad.

"Laren, could you please send out the pings now that the ECs have been booted?" Markos asked.

Laren went to the AVR control panel and loaded the necessary holo screens.

"Pings are sent," she said. "The Redshift program is initiating the local virtual environment."

The eight convex chassis glowed bluish-white to signify their readiness. Other AVR bays like this one were aboard Ascentia, but due to the high-profile nature of the mission, all users were logged out. Eventually, a chirp sounded, indicating the Redshift program was ready.

"You have a 200 GU radius mapped out," Laren said. "Kal Dera should be well within that range."

"Oh yeah, plenty of room to blow stuff up," Gareth said.

"Combat Mode won't be activated," Markos said. "This is a research mission."

Audible groans resounded from the crew.

Laren grabbed Markos' arm and pulled him over to her.

"Please, be careful out there."

"Babe, I'm literally not going anywhere," he said, gesturing to the EC.

"I know that, but … we just don't know what is causing the distortion or why. It could be—"

"Yeah, you're right. I'll keep my field of view as wide as possible. Promise. Plus, you're watching over me like my own personal guardian angel."

She nodded. They kissed again before Markos lifted himself onto the EC. The chassis leaned back slightly, a curved lens closing over him like an egg. His specially made redsuit reacted to the bed's frame, lifting him to hover and twist around completely while the machine was on. Markos always thought of it as anti-gravity, but he knew the millions of miniature magnets kept him afloat.

Laren stood in front of the wall of screens. From there, she observed everything the drivers saw, the same as crew members on Ascentia's bridge.

It'd been a while since Markos last used Redshift and, this time, he wasn't poking around a random asteroid belt in search of additional resources. He'd finally be a part of a historic moment for his people, something he could be proud of. Something to tell his little scout when she grew old enough for bedtime stories.

As he waited, Markos checked his controls in the 4D environment. His fellow drivers' faces floated in the upper part of his view. They were considered the best players on board the cruiser. Their avatars had incredibly high-ranked gear and could take on whatever the AVR world threw at them.

Vayto, a thin black-haired man, gave a thumbs-up to Markos via the feed. The others followed: Merium, Yan, Greynos, Sapp, and Triln. Gareth feigned a snore, his eyes closed. Markos ignored him.

"Alright, Bridge, can you hear me?" Markos asked.

"Yes, loud and clear," Commander Clark's voice came over their comms. "Although there seems to be some interference?" Markos manually muted Gareth. "Never mind. Whatever you did fixed it."

"Great, sir. We're ready for the go-ahead," Markos said, making eye contact with winking Gareth.

"You're free to begin, Markos."

Markos nodded to the other drivers, their feeds disappearing from his view. He hit Start, and the lens around him turned black. Specks of white dotted the utter darkness as the virtual world generated. A small blue light appeared in the distance. It grew larger, speeding toward him, then halted as a row of blocks morphed into the game's title, "Redshift." The letters alternated between every primary color before blasting back in the direction they had come, the color bleeding into a uniform red before fading away.

The holo screen went from black to a clean rendition of the AVR Bay where they had loaded into their ECs. Markos subconsciously looked for Laren where she had been standing, but she wasn't there. This was standard for Redshift, as the system removed non-users from the final rendering for legal reasons.

"Laren?" Markos asked.

"Yes, I'm here," she said. "Everything is looking good from an equipment standpoint. How is the system responding to the latest update?"

"Let me see," he said, stepping out of the EC.

The others exited their chassis as well. With Combat Mode locked, their characters were exact copies of themselves in real life or IRL. They still wore their redsuits, now with helmets closed around their heads.

"Wow, I almost can't tell the difference," Markos said.

"Almost?" Merium said. "There should be zero difference. I read through all of the latest patch notes. It's the most advanced version ever."

"This is incredible," Yan said. "I can't believe the game has come this far." The short man pulled up an inventory only he could see, swiping through it. "Markos wasn't lying. None of my gear is available. Bummer."

"Official business," Markos said. "You know the rules. Now, let's get out there."

A giant airlock in the AVR Bay didn't exist IRL but had been programmed into the game for ease of deployment from the cruiser. Reaching the panel that controlled the door to space, Markos checked with the other drivers one last time.

"Everyone ready?"

"Been ready for the last fifteen minutes," Gareth said. "Let's hurry up."

"Weren't you just sleeping?" Tiln asked.

Markos took the banter as a "yes" and triggered the airlock. The door opened, and the air was sucked out along with the drivers, their bodies tumbling into space. Redshift was programmed to simulate reality in every way, especially real-life physics. Laren stood in the calm bay with eight drivers floating in their ECs, nothing exciting besides what she saw on the screens.

The redsuit's air jets popped and hissed, auto-stabilizing the drivers' orientation to Ascentia. Within seconds, they were all upright in relation to the space cruiser, which gleamed a brilliant white against the infinite backdrop, like a star all its own, harboring the essential components of life.

Markos tapped a blinking icon on his forearm. His redsuit recognized he had left the ship and required a vehicle augment known as a jacket. Eight capsules blasted from beneath Ascentia's hull and shot toward them. The jackets were silent in their approach, but not for lack of speed.

"Brace yourselves," Markos said. He faced away from the vehicle augment rocketing toward him.

The encroaching jackets snapped open like wings, revealing a hollow interior for the drivers to fit into. Markos' redsuit jets coordinated with the jacket for a smooth boarding experience. He pulled himself inside. The doors closed, and the locks engaged, sound returning with chirps from the computers and a low hum of the engine.

"Jacket secured," Markos said. He opened his inventory and swiped down to vehicle skins available in this mode. Markos chose the only option, the standard Eagle-10 space fighter. However, he opted for deep crimson paint.

"Show off," Merium said, pulling up beside him. Her jacket was still the standard flat gray. A few others changed their colors, too. Gareth sported a particularly obnoxious yellow.

"Bridge, drivers are ready to enter the distortion," Markos said.

"Roger that, Markos," Commander Clark said. "We'll see everything you see here on our screens. Godspeed."

Markos grabbed the two levers that functioned as thrust and steering. For a moment, he'd forgotten almost none of this was real and he was still floating in the EC onboard Ascentia next to his wife. He supposed that was the intent behind Redshift, a game designed to be more than a game, a tool for corporate to ensure safe passage of their greatest assets during space travel.

"Drivers," he said. "Punch it."

Markos laid into the thrust and shot forward with the others in pursuit, their colors streaking through the midnight black.

* * *

The bridge had opted to view the mission through Markos' HUD, so everything within his field of view surrounded them on the massive screens. The room was muted so they could speak freely without Markos having to hear.

"When will we know they've crossed the threshold?" Clark asked.

"Sir, ALI shows that the distortion begins at 2 GUs, or approximately six minutes at their current speed," Sandy said.

"I want to tell them when they're close, so they aren't blindsided."

"Of course, Commander. What do you think it will look like when they cross?"

"Speculating that would be like imagining what goes through a Scav's brain to justify their actions as morally righteous. Nigh impossible."

At this, Rob perked up.

"Yeah, only one thing should be going through a Scav's brain," he said. "Right, Commander?"

Clark raised an eyebrow but didn't encourage the man. He wasn't too fond of folks trying to win him over by appealing to his past trauma. Clark was here to do a job, not make friends. He'd learned that lesson the hard way.

"Three minutes, sir."

Sandy looked at him with concern after giving the update. She'd likely read past mission logs and knew what he'd gone through: the calls for help and the number of dead. Space was isolating enough on its own but drifting on a broken ship with no one to keep you company created a whole different nightmare he was still trying to wake up from.

Clark stared at the red stars glowing brighter as Markos approached. Something bugged him, but he couldn't scratch what itched just out of mental reach.

"Sandy, earlier, you said the starlight was traveling away from us," he said. "Isn't that what is known as redshift?"

"Yes, sir," she said. "It's the increased length of light waves, and since that end of the visible spectrum is red, we call it redshift. It's also the origin of the AVR program's name, which we co-opted for space exploration. It's how the game functions fundamentally: measuring and mapping a 3D environment using electromagnetic readings, light waves, and radiological fluctuations across a scanned physical space."

"So, in a way, we're creating a distortion of our own when we boot up the Redshift program?"

"Not exactly. We're not altering the visible spectrum of light, not that we can see anyway."

"What do you mean?"

"Well, I'm not an expert on Redshift technology, sir. You'll want clarification from the augment team, but I believe the spatial pings send out a detectable level of radiation, which could theoretically be seen by someone looking for such disturbances."

That has to be it, Clark thought.

"How far is Markos from the distortion?"

"Less than a minute, sir."

"Open comms."

"Yes, sir."

"Markos, do you read?"

"Hey, Commander. Loud and clear."

"Halt the mission. This is possibly a trap. Someone seems to be imitating our technology in a way we do not yet understand."

They watched as Markos' feed slowed to a stop. He passed the order to the others, and their fighters floated around him in a half-circle.

"Sir, with all due respect, we're in a virtual environment. Isn't the purpose of Redshift to prevent harm? What could be the trouble?"

Clark leaned on his cane, staring at the Bal Aldorax crystal set into its grip.

"Yes, Markos. I know it seems ridiculous. I—We just need some more time to understand what we're dealing with."

The room gasped and murmured as new information appeared on the spectral readers' screens. Sandy looked up from her computer and cleared her throat.

"Commander, I hate to be the bearer of bad news," she said. "But it's too late for second thoughts."

"What?"

"The distortion is expanding at great speed."

"Markos, get out of there. Turn off Redshift. Do whatever —"

"Sir," Sandy said, "They're already inside the distortion, and so are we."

They stared at each other in unblinking silence.

"Um, Bridge, are you seeing this?" Markos said.

Everyone on the bridge looked up. A planet filled a large portion of the center screen. Kal Dera was not the lush, green world they had once cataloged.

It was quite the opposite.

* * *

The drivers approached the planet at breakneck speed, the orange sphere filling Markos' HUD. A reddish-black torrent scraped across the planet's surface, moving in one direction. The massive storm gave Markos the impression of being insatiably hungry, feasting on itself and spitting out remnants to scatter upon the gale-force winds.

When entering the upper atmosphere, the jacket's outer shell glowed red hot. Markos wasn't supposed to feel simulated heat, as it wouldn't benefit a driver to suffer, but a phantom warmth enveloped him as flames plumed around the front of the nose and threatened to swallow the vehicle.

With further instruction from the commander, the drivers were to follow through with their mission of scouting out Kal Dera's surface for any signs of the source of the distortion field, which emanated from the planet. If none could be found, they would prepare for a return trip to their home system.

The squadron entered the initial layer of cloud cover, everything growing dark around them. Triln and Merium shot past Markos at full speed. They raced through lightning-filled clouds to reach the surface. He slowed, studying the storm's chemistry. Purple, and sometimes green, tendrils of electricity sparked around him, bolts zipping in every direction. Several connected with the jacket, but nothing happened. Markos was sure if it had been IRL, he'd be dead from the explosive discharge.

"Merium, did you see that?" Triln asked.

"I think so."

"What's going on down there?" Clark asked. "Tell me everything."

"I think something just flew past us," Merium added. "Whoa, pull up, Triln, pull up."

Triln screamed before her feed went blank and disconnected from the program. A blur shot past Markos on his left. He blinked. Then, two more on his right.

Was he hallucinating?

"Merium, what's happening?"

"Markos, the storm clouds connect with the surface. Pull up now!"

As she said this, a red dune appeared dead ahead. Markos pulled the steering lever to the side, barely missing the arching formation. He'd almost become a thousand tiny pieces.

"Laren, is Triln okay? What's happening? Environmental deaths should be disabled for this mission."

"Triln is fine. She's getting out of the EC now." Markos heard Triln cursing over the comms in the background as Laren spoke to him. "It seems the system is no longer responding to her inputs. I'm not sure how to explain it yet, Markos. But something is interfering with the in-game mechanics of Redshift."

Markos discovered an incredible archway where acid wind had molded sand over time to form a great alcove underneath. He pulled his vehicle under the arch's ceiling and hovered there momentarily. Amidst the planetary chaos, it felt oddly serene. More rocks flew through an orange haze of sand and dirt. A boulder three times larger than his jacket hurdled past, bouncing off the ground like a toy ball.

"Bridge, this planet is not viable," Markos said. "The sheer force of the storm winds has altered the surface, ruining any compatibility for life. As for the source of the distortion, I have nothing to —"

Markos cut off as more screams erupted. Yan's feed disappeared, followed by Greynos'. In both instances, a dark figure engulfed their screens.

"Squadron, status report," Markos said.

"Something is chasing us," Vayto said.

"And they are not happy," Gareth added.

"Laren, we have hostiles," Markos said. "Why are my drivers getting taken out by hostiles?"

"I checked," she said. "Combat Mode is off. There should be no enemies in-game."

"That's because we're not in control here," Clark said. "If my assumption is correct, the distortion has augmented our perception and how we interact with the environment. In other words, you're no longer operating in your game. You're now in theirs. We all are."

Comms fell quiet for a moment as reality set in for everyone. Markos wasn't sure what to say or if it would change anything if he did.

It didn't take long for a new threat to emerge.

"We have two UAPs leaving Kal Dera's atmosphere, heading straight for the Ascentia," Laren said, raising the alarm.

Markos exited the calm archway, aiming the vehicle up to leave the planet's surface behind. Merium did the same, her blinking dot on his HUD rising with his out of the storm. Gareth and Vayto roiled in the blistering winds with a foreign entity tailing them in close pursuit.

* * *

Two obsidian figures rose from Kal Dera. The drivers who had died in-game stood behind Laren, watching everything unfold on the holo screens. Four feeds remained: two showing a frantic chase for survival in the storm clouds and two rocketing up behind the enemy.

"Markos, there's no point in remaining in AVR. You should disconnect, and we'll figure out how to deal with them from the bridge," Laren said.

Markos didn't respond.

"Commander, are you attempting to hail the inbound UAPs?" she asked.

When Clark opened comms again, a crash of yelling voices flooded the room, "— and get those defensive cannons ready. Are the shields up?"

"Laren," he said, returning his attention to her. "I don't think there's time for diplomacy. I'm doing all I can to keep us safe. If I must attack first, then so be it."

She considered countering him, but he was right. They couldn't risk their lives, not when they didn't understand the beings' motives.

Then, she saw one up close on Markos' feed. Red and piercing eyes tracked him as Markos shot past. The being had a humanoid body that seemed exaggerated and alien. Their hardened skin, or armor, was pitch black, light barely reflecting off its oily surface.

Markos circled to get a better angle. The alien raised a long tentacle jutting from its hunched back over its head to aim at him, proving it indeed saw her husband in the program despite him resting in the nearby EC. This being, whatever it was, did not operate by the rules of the known universe. Or, rather, it had created its own rules, as the commander suggested.

Without warning, the being fired from its tentacle, a purplish beam blasting through the nose of Markos' vehicle. The jacket's shell fell apart around him, sending him flying through floating shrapnel. His feed went haywire as he spun through the vacuum of space. The redsuit's air jets finally reoriented him and his camera, which showed the being already aiming at Merium.

Clark must have taken the alien's attack as first blood since two Bal cannons fired with all their blue, destructive glory. The second creature, the one still charging toward Ascentia, took the brunt of both beams, but from Markos' feed, Laren saw it took no damage. It had braced for the impact, forming an energy shield to protect itself. Their cannons continued to fire, keeping it distracted.

Gareth's feed suddenly went dark, and he jumped out of his EC, seething.

"Stars!" he exclaimed. "What was that thing?

Gareth marched up to the holo screens where the team huddled.

"Why won't the system let me log back in?" he asked. "Hey, Laren, are the comms still connected?"

"Yes, Gareth, everyone can hear you," Laren said.

"Vayto," Gareth yelled. "Did it work?"

"Yes, I think so," Vayto said, dodging lightning bolts as he climbed in altitude, chasing after the being. "It's definitely injured from the explosion. It's not as fast as before."

"Cash of crystals," Gareth said. "Markos, I just slammed my jacket into one of those things head-on. Don't ask me how or why but attacking them in Redshift affects them. You thinking what I'm thinking?"

The same being that blew up Markos' jacket blasted Merium to smithereens. She sat up in the AVR Bay, cursing.

"Sure am," Markos said. "Laren, switch Redshift into Combat Mode. Give Vayto and me access to all our gear. This just might work."

"That's insane," Laren said. "Just disconnect. What if something goes wrong?"

"Look, everyone is with you in the bay, right?" he said. "Nothing is going to happen to me. We don't have time. It'll work, I promise."

Laren relented, opening the system's menu. A series of boxes showed available mods to change Redshift's gameplay. She hovered over an unchecked box that toggled in-game fighting.

"Hurry," Markos said.

Laren looked up and saw the first being aiming its glowing tentacle toward the Ascentia. She clicked the box.

Markos opened his inventory to find his in-game items populating. He selected his favorite loadout with the highest-rated gear. Laren and the other drivers could only watch helplessly as humanity officially engaged in its first-ever interspecies conflict, facilitated, for better or worse, by what was technically and functionally a video game.

* * *

Markos' redsuit morphed into a sleek suit of metallic plating. His in-game HUD went from a basic display to one with distances, power stats, target locks, and more. Two massive energy swords extended from the forearms of his new armor, their hum providing Markos with relative comfort.

He shot forward with the power of Bal jets now on his back. He became a red blur, streaking through space like a comet. The first being charging for an attack had no time to react. Markos slammed through the tentacle at high speed, severing it with an outward thrust of both swords. Purplish blood splattered across his visor as he rocketed past.

The AVR bay cheered in his headphones. It had actually worked. Markos and Vayto now had a fighting chance to save Ascentia. They were no longer helpless prey.

The tentacle-less being faced Markos, its eyes flaring brighter. A number indicating its level hovered over its head, but it was blurred out for some reason, along with what he thought was a health bar. He tried to access their codex page, which would reveal crucial information. However, it was blank.

Were they preventing him from seeing their weaknesses?

With two outstretched arms, the being's sleek body bubbled up like tar, stringy tendrils of ooze floating outward in zero gravity. A sudden jolt sent slender tethers spiraling toward Markos from all sides. He tried to swipe at them with his energy swords, but they quickly overwhelmed him, their sticky consistency rendering his attempts to defend himself useless. Each of his limbs became stuck in place, unmovable.

The being pulled him closer. Immobilized by the tendrils, a sudden wave of exhaustion came over him. He realized the enemy's physical makeup was likely causing a negative status effect to take hold.

"Vayto, I need some help."

"I'm a bit busy, friend," Vayto said.

Markos now saw that Vayto engaged the other injured being in hand-to-hand combat using his signature metal-spiked gloves.

"Desperate times," Markos mumbled.

He disengaged his swords and selected his "Fiery Reign" ability. Its cooldown duration was so long that it was basically a one-time use in a fight like this. But he had no choice but to give it his all.

The redsuit glowed orange as it heated up to the equivalent of molten lava. The stringy, black tendrils constricting him popped and hissed as the rapidly rising temperature of the armor burned them away. Markos felt his energy returning, the status effect fading.

He burst free from the tar-like trap and decided to take a page from Vayto's book by closing the remaining distance on the tentacle-less being. His jets got him there in the blink of an eye, and he used his still-heated fists to pummel the being with several well-placed blows. Each time his knuckles landed, the enemy's armor bent inward from the impact.

The ability soon ended, and his suit cooled back to normal. With the being now dazed, Markos selected his second favorite weapon from his inventory: a laser cannon. Its hulking shape materialized over his right shoulder, and he grabbed the pommel triggers with both hands. The barrel of the cannon began absorbing tiny particles of light, a ball of energy forming at its center.

"Let's see you block this."

He fired. The being did manage to throw up its blue shield just in time for the pillar of energy to connect with it. However, it wasn't strong enough to hold back the blast, and the shield shattered. The beam engulfed it in a wall of light and disintegrated it into a thousand pieces.

"Markos, you defeated one," Laren said.

"Looks like I did."

"Heck yeah! Now that's what I'm talking about," Gareth said.

"I'm only reading one more enemy combatant," Laren said. "Vayto has also been victorious in his fight."

"Two versus one shouldn't be too bad," Markos said, looking around. "But where did it go?"

"Markos, look out," Vayto said.

A beam of purple energy tore past him. At first, he thought himself lucky but soon realized that it hadn't aimed for him. The beam pierced the side of Ascentia with such force that it exited through the other end of the cruiser.

"No!"

Markos froze as he watched the cruiser roll off-kilter like a fatally harpooned whale giving up on life. Pockets of explosions erupted, debris scattering, leaking its lifeblood out into the sea of infinite death.

"Laren!" he shouted. "Laren, can you hear me?"

A response came, but not from Ascentia. It belonged to an icy voice, one that sounded like a static whisper in his headphones. One that wasn't human.

"WE … HEAR … YOU …" the being said. "WE … ARE … SEN. WE … ARE … ETERNAL."

Vayto arrived next to Markos.

"Look," he said. "It's doing something with the others."

Markos ripped his eyes away from the damaged cruiser to understand what Vayto was talking about. His HUD locked onto the third being going through some sort of transformation. Shredded remnants of the two defeated beings pooled around its hunched form, its armor absorbing black ooze and rippling into a lighter grey, spikes extending outward from its joints and back. Once it finished, Markos recognized that it had evolved into something … *else*.

"It's up to us, Vayto. The survivors on Ascentia won't make it unless we kill this thing."

Vayto struck his fist into his palm.

"Good thing I like to play on the highest difficulty."

Markos grinned and nodded.

"Let's finish this."

* * *

Clark woke to a deafening alarm. He wished the sound wasn't so familiar. But it had returned as if it had always been there, muted and waiting for him to turn on the volume. Another vessel, another attack, and more lives lost under his command.

He tried to get up, but his legs wouldn't budge. Clark's back implant had been damaged when he fell back into the consoles. He searched for his cane. Instead, his eyes locked on a body that lay unmoving.

"Sandy," Clark said with muted horror.

Clark dragged himself across the floor. Sparks flew out from cracked screens above him, which no longer streamed Markos' feed. Some sections continued to flash between footage from the MSCs on the outer hull and a blank white background, creating a strobe-like effect.

He reached Sandy after an agonizing crawl. Blood leaked down her forehead. Clark didn't want to move her without knowing the full extent of her injuries. He checked her pulse but couldn't find one.

Clark cursed and slammed a fist down on the floor. A few crewmembers cried and yelled fearfully on the bridge; others were clinging to life. What could he do for them in his injured state? Why had he been the one to lead this mission? Why had he taken the job?

A hand fell on his shoulder.

"Sir, are you okay? I found this on the floor."

Rob offered Clark the small black cylinder, the cane having retracted. A simple gesture, one that reminded him of his purpose.

Survive.

"Thank you, Rob."

Clark took the device from Rob. He rolled to his side and lifted his jacket, leveling the device near his implant. Tiny wires extended and began to work autonomously out of sight. An intense sensation returned to Clark's lower half, and he welcomed it.

That great cresting wave of beautiful, tingling pain.

"ALI, give me a status update."

"Commander ... cruiser has sustained ... critical damage," ALI's voice stuttered in and out. "One AVR bay has been destroyed ... I've isolated the leak … internal atmosphere regulation is under control. Three of five Bal Aldorax crystals … are unstable. Long-distance space travel is not possible … major repairs are needed … three hours and twenty-three minutes until catastrophic system failure."

* * *

Laren woke to cauterized destruction on a scale she'd never seen. Hot air mixed with thin oxygen. Smoke filled her vision. Gareth and Merium were beside her with smiles that didn't reach their eyes.

"Thank God," Gareth said.

"We must get you to safety," Merium added.

Laren touched her stomach as she sat up. She wasn't in pain, she wasn't hurt. But she realized some of the others were not so lucky. Tears came unbidden.

"Where is Markos?" Laren asked.

Gareth looked at Merium with wide eyes.

"Laren, the Bal crystal nearest us is unstable. There's no time. We have to leave."

"What aren't you telling me?" she replied. "What's happened?"

Gareth moved to his other knee to give her a view of the EC harboring her husband's body. It had been destroyed by falling debris. He wasn't within view, but she knew no one could survive that amount of metal heaped atop them.

Laren cried out and tried to get to her feet, but Gareth stopped her.

"He's not gone … not *completely*," Merium said.

"What do you mean?" Laren asked incredulously.

Merium pointed to the last functioning holo screen. It still contained Markos' live feed of him fighting the third being in Redshift. He was alive … in the program.

"I don't understand how it's possible," Gareth said.

"It's not our game anymore, it's theirs," Laren whispered. She scrambled to her feet, stumbled to the screen, and pressed the comms button. "Markos, can you hear me?"

"Laren? Thank God, you're alive."

She watched as Vayto stepped in to fight the strange, powerful being. They appeared more evenly matched than before. But it was two-on-one, and they hadn't won yet. Markos' feed showed him looking back at the damaged Ascentia.

Laren glanced at the pile of debris once again, and fresh tears streamed down her smudged cheeks.

"You promised."

"What?"

"You said you'd come back to me."

There was a pause.

"I'm right here," Markos said, confused. "I'm not going anywhere."

* * *

Clark placed Sandy's lifeless body on his bed and knelt to pray over her. Afterward, he sat down and rested his back against the bed's frame. Contemplating what to do next.

"ALI, can the cruiser be piloted in its current state?"

"Yes, Commander."

"How long would it take to reach Kal Dera?"

"Based on my current projections, it will take nearly two hours and thirteen minutes."

"If we land the cruiser under one of those arches, could we survive?"

"Theoretically, yes. However, Ascentia was built for space travel. The cruiser will be incapable of returning to space once you land on the planet's surface."

"It's our only choice."

ALI was quiet for a moment.

"To avoid destruction, you are correct, Commander."

"As the commander of this vessel, I mean to avoid such a fate. Land Ascentia on Kal Dera, ALI."

"Yes, Commander."

A slight jolt, and the cruiser began to move to its final destination. Clark looked up at the transparent ceiling of his quarters. The distance between him and his home felt farther away than ever.

"ALI."

"Yes, Commander?"

"Play the sounds of the ocean."

* * *

Markos watched Vayto log out of Redshift. They had defeated the third being, but it fled before they could kill it. The being called its kind "Sen." He wondered how many were still out there, watching, waiting to strike.

Laren finally explained to him how his physical body was destroyed in the EC when the Sen's attack struck the cruiser. Yet, his mind remained conscious inside the program. With all the other anomalies, they could only assume the Sen's influence had affected the code in a certain way; a glitch, some had called it.

Markos stood alone in the AVR bay of the downed Ascentia. He'd heard they had been forced to land on Kal Dera's surface. An unimaginable compromise to live another day. Maybe they could escape in time.

Laren loaded into Redshift. She ran into his embrace, and they held each other tight. Markos let her go and crouched down. She smiled.

"How's my little scout?"

"Safe. Thanks to you."

"Good. I've sure got a story to tell her when she's old enough to hear it."

He stood to kiss her. She reciprocated. He hoped their kiss and renewed embrace would never end, but it did. Laren's brow furrowed, and her eyes darted across his features, examining him.

"They say the emergency broadcast frequency won't extend beyond the distortion. We don't have a way to contact the others. We're stuck here."

Markos swallowed hard and took a step back.

"Well, I won't let my death be in vain. I'll find a way to get us home if it's the last thing I do."

Laren nodded.

"My personal guardian angel?"

"Always."

Winston Malone is a USAF veteran who is fond of speculative fiction and poetry. He founded Storyletter XPress Publishing LLC to support and publish quality independent writing. He also owns and operates the Enchanted Books bookstore in Rio Rancho, New Mexico. You can follow his work at storyletter.substack.com and havek.substack.com.

Also by John Coon

Among Hidden Stars

A tyrannical ruler seeks an ancient relic that imparts god-like powers and use it as a world-conquering weapon. Will a rebel couple find the hidden relic first and finally defeat their oppressor's reign?

Book no. 3 in the *Alien People Chronicles* science fiction adventure series.